G000137588

The
STARFISH
method

An Unexpected Lovers Prequel

JB HELLER

STARFISH- A BILLIONAIRE ROMCOM

Copyright © 2019 by JB Heller

Published by- Author JB Heller
Cover Design by- Tall Story Designs
Editing by- Creating Ink
Proofreading by- Jenn Lockwood Editing
Formatted by – JeBDesigns

CHAPTER ONE

HANNAH

ONCE UPON A TIME, THERE WAS A GIRL WHO BELIEVED in true love and happily-ever-afters.

That girl was me. Notice the past tense there: was . . . Yeah, I let go of that fairy-tale kind of hope a long time ago. Don't get me wrong; I want to believe. I really do. But there's only so much heartbreak a girl can take before she starts to question her fundamental beliefs.

For instance, my first boyfriend back in ninth grade, Toby Miller (insert dreamy sigh), ticked all my boxes. Handsome? Yep. Funny? Uh-huh. Charming? Yeppers. Taller than me? You bet ya. And smart? Bingo. Unfortunately for me, I was not the only girl he was wooing with his swoon-worthiness.

Next, we have Bryan Godfrey. After being burned by Toby and his Lothario ways, I added honest to my list of requirements. And Bryan, bless him, was honest to a fault. So honest he felt the need to inform me of every failing I possessed. But don't worry. He did it in a very charming way. So charmingly, in fact, that it took me a while to realize he was actually insulting me.

Then there was Grey Mathers, Will Carson, Aiden Fairmont, Alex Norman, and the list goes on. You get where I'm going with this, right? A string of unsuccessful relationships left me jaded and—for lack of a better word—hopeless.

So, I devised a plan to keep my banged-up heart safe from all the douche-canoes in the world. I call it The Starfish Method. It's really quite genius. You see, I still have needs as a woman, and I very much like companionship, so dropping out of the dating game altogether just wasn't an option for me.

In order to continue reaping the benefits of a relationship without becoming too invested, I only date each man for four months. Then, I give myself a month or two break before diving back into the dating pool again.

The tricky part is getting rid of the current boytoy without him knowing I'm trying to get rid of him. That's where The Starfish Method comes into play. At the three-month mark, I take a step back in being an active participant in the sex department and implement my secret weapon: I lie there like a starfish, limbs spread so the deed can successfully be done and mostly enjoyed by both parties. But it's not great, you know?

It's so simple, it's genius.

After a couple of weeks of this, he (the current lover) will become bored and ultimately invent a reason to break it off within my four-month time frame. It hasn't failed me yet, and I've been employing this method for four years.

"You're insane. You know that, right?" Amy, my BFF since our diaper days, says as I pop another fry into my mouth.

I shrug as I chew. "So you keep telling me."

She snatches the bowl out of my grasp as I reach for another stick of potatoey goodness. I glare. "Dude, is there a reason you're taking your life into your hands right now?"

Her brows bunch in a frown. "This is serious. Taking away the carbs is the only way to make you listen."

I blow my bangs out of my eyes and look to the heavens, silently begging for patience. When I level her with my stare again, she's clutching the bowl of fries to her chest. "Give them back and we can talk. There's no need to hold my food hostage."

She snorts. "Right. I'm not falling for that again. We talk first, then I'll return your precious grease sticks."

Crossing my arms over my chest, I retort, "Well, get on with it then. I'm hungry."

Amy clears her throat then straightens her shoulders. "I think you should have held on to Brent. He's so nice, and he treated you like a damn princess. Don't even get me started on the way he looked at you like you were the most amazing thing on this Earth."

I drop my head to the tabletop. "You should date him if you like him so much," I grumble.

"Maybe if I'd met him first, I would have. But that's just gross. I don't want a bar of his pork sword after it's already impaled my bestie." She dry heaves then shakes her head. "Besides, he was crazy about you. Can't you give him a chance? Like, a real one this time?"

Sitting forward, I let my bravado go and get real. "I don't think I have it in me to give anyone more of myself than I already do. My system works for me. It keeps my heart safe while still meeting all my needs. Brent is a great guy, otherwise I wouldn't have hooked up with him in the first place. But you and I both know there's always an expiration date on the 'perfect guy' routine. I get out before I get hurt."

Amy's frown deepens. "But what if it's not a routine? I think he's genuine."

I grin. "That's where my system comes in. If he was truly crazy about me, not just the great sex, he wouldn't have broken it off with me. But he did. You can't fault The Starfish Method. In the last four years, not one of the guys I've dated has stuck around to try to work things out."

"Life isn't only about sex, you know," she grumbles.

"Ames." I sigh. "I know that. But think about it; if Brent really liked me, for more than a good lay, he would have stuck around."

After a full minute of silence, Amy finally nods. "Yeah, I guess you're right. I just really liked this one. I thought for sure he'd blow your stupid starfish out of the water."

I chuckle and reach across the space between us, snatching my bowl of fries out of her arms. "Maybe one day I'll meet the unicorn of men, and he'll stick it to me so good it won't matter what position we're in as long as we're boning."

SAM

CAMILLE HANDS ME A SMALL BLACK-AND-WHITE picture on gloss paper, and I stare at it, confused. "What is this?"

She smiles and slaps my shoulder playfully. "What do you think it is, silly? It's our baby. We made a baby together, Samuel. Isn't it wonderful?" Her blue eyes mist with unshed tears as she speaks.

I go back to staring at the picture. A baby? She told me she was on the pill. . . and I wrapped it every single time we've been together despite her repeatedly mentioning that I didn't need to.

"Say something, Samuel. You're scaring me," Camille says, planting her ass on the edge of my desk in front of me.

"I'm not exactly sure how this happened, Camille."

She laughs, and it's so fake and irritating it grates on my nerves.

Shaking my head, I hand her back the sonogram picture. "That's not what I meant. I know how it happened, obviously. I just don't understand. We've been using two forms of contraception."

"Neither of which are one hundred percent

guaranteed to work. I think this is a sign that we're supposed to be together, Samuel. You, me, and this baby." She rests a hand over her still-flat stomach, a single tear spilling onto her cheek. "We're going to be a family. The wedding will have to be soon, though. I don't want to be showing in the pictures."

I stare at her like she's lost her damn mind. Because clearly, she has, if she thinks I'm going to marry her when we've only been seeing each other for five months.

She doesn't seem to notice the expression on my face as she reaches out a hand and cups my cheek. "You've made me the happiest woman in the world, Samuel. I will be the best wife and mother you could ever dream of."

Okay, no. "Listen. . ." I take her hand from my cheek and hold it between my own. "I will be there for you every step of the way. All the ultrasounds and doctors' appointments. I'll even be at every recital or football game without fail. But what I will not be doing is marrying you."

Camille yanks her hand out of my grip, rears it back, and slaps me across the face. "I am carrying your child! Of course we need to get married. How could you disrespect me like this, Samuel?"

I close my eyes and rub the bridge of my nose. "I'm not disrespecting you. I just told you I'll take care of you and the child. But we don't even know each other that well. And I'm sorry to say this— especially right now—but I had planned on ending things between us."

Her eyes flare. "I know you were, you moron!" she seethes and pushes to her feet. Stalking around the desk, she lets out what can only be called a screech as she slams her palms on the marble surface. "I went to all the trouble of getting that damn sonogram picture and you still won't commit. You have a problem, Samuel English."

My head kicks to the side. "What did you just say?"

Camille straightens, seemingly having realized what she's let slip.

"You're not pregnant, are you? You thought you'd come in here, tell me we're having a baby, and I'd drop to one knee and propose. If you knew me at all, you'd know there's no way I would do that." I shake my head. "And for your information, a child doesn't need their parents to be married—it needs their parents to be happy. And nothing would make me more miserable than sharing the rest of my life with a conniving bitch like you. Now get out."

IT HAS BEEN A LONG-ASS DAY, AND I'M DONE WITH IT. I'm kicking back with my feet on my desk, sipping a whiskey, when my cousin Tom wanders in and drops into the seat across from me.

"Whiskey in the office? Did I miss something? I thought the merger with Svendenson was going well?" he says, watching me cautiously.

Scrubbing a hand over my face, I groan then lean forward before dropping my feet to the floor and bracing my forearms on my desk. "Camille faked a pregnancy."

"I'm sorry, what?"

I take a deep breath as my fingertips strum over the cool marble beneath them. "She came in to see me at lunch today. Figured I'd marry her if she was pregnant. Went as far as to produce a fake sonogram."

Tom's eyes widen. "Are you fucking serious? Bitch is crazy. You've only been boning for a couple of months."

Shrugging, I glance at my hands. "Apparently, being heir to the English fortune is reason enough to marry me. Anyway, the condensed version is I told her I'd support her and the child, be an active parent, but no fucking way was I marrying her after a few months. She then lost her shit and accidently confessed."

Tom sneers. "I've had some pretty desperate dames, but none of them have gone *that* far to try to lock me down. What is wrong with these women?"

"It's the world we live in. They're raised to be money-hungry bitches. More money equals more power and prestige. I'm done with psychos trying to trap me for nothing more than what my name represents."

"I get that. But where are you going to find a woman who doesn't give a shit who you are? Seriously, Sam, it's what these women do. It's how they're wired: find a man—trap the man—consume the man's happiness," Tom states matter-of-factly.

I laugh. "Surely there is a woman out there who doesn't know who I am and who will happily wave me off when our time is up. Right now, I'd settle for a few months of good, old-fashioned fun without having to take out a restraining order at the end of it."

"I think this day calls for a stiff drink—or five," Tom suggests.

I nod, holding out my now empty whiskey glass. "I'm way ahead of you, cousin."

He shakes his head. "Not here. That's just depressing."

"Okay, but I'm not going to the club. I can't stomach another night being surrounded by social climbers trying to dig their claws into me."

"I know a place." Tom grins then pushes to his feet, and I follow him out of my office to the elevators at the end of the hall.

"Your car will be waiting, Mr. English," my secretary calls from behind me.

Peering over my shoulder, I give her a nod. "Thanks, Mary. See you on Monday. Have a fun weekend with those grandkids of yours."

Fifteen minutes later, my car pulls up outside a bar I don't recognize. I glance at Tom and he smiles. "I bought it last month. It was time to do something different. I'm bored, man, and you know what I do when I get bored."

Yeah, I do. He spends money—lots of it.

I survey the exterior of the building from the sidewalk. The name is splashed across the wall in a big, neon-blue script: The Aquarium. It's clean, in a good area, and there is a line of people already gathered out in front. We, of course, skip it, walking straight through the doors without a backward glance at the people waiting in the heat of the night.

"Interesting name for a bar," I murmur as we walk along a darkened corridor toward a set of heavy, blue velvet curtains.

Tom's grin widens. "It'll make sense in a minute."

A hostess greets us as we approach the curtains, the muffled sound of the music seeping through just slightly.

"Mr. English, so good to see you again. I'll have your booth prepared immediately. Will there be anyone else joining this party tonight, sir?" the woman croons.

"No, thank you, Mira. Only my cousin Sam and myself this evening."

Mira nods and presses a button on a small headset I didn't even notice she was wearing, murmuring something then smiling brightly at Tom again. "Would you like me to escort you through tonight, Mr. English?"

The corner of Tom's mouth hooks in a smirk as he shakes his head slightly. "I think we can manage. Thank you, Mira."

Without another word, she tugs one of the heavy curtains aside to allow us entry. Tom gestures for me to go first, and as I step over the threshold, I'm taken aback by the scene around me. Now the name makes perfect sense.

"Amazing, right?" Tom says, clasping a hand over my shoulder. And all I can do is nod.

CHAPTER TWO

SAM

"Jesus Christ!" I just about yell as a shark swims right over my fucking head. A shark. Like a real, live, man-eating shark.

"I know." He chuckles. "See why I had to buy this place? I've never seen anything like it." Then he gives my back a shove, moving me forward through a glass tunnel.

"It's a literal aquarium," I say in wonderment.

"Yep, and a bar. What could be more relaxing than admiring fish while you drink?"

True enough, I suppose. I have a fish tank built into the wall at my office and two at home. It helps me decompress, watching their sleek bodies glide through the water so effortlessly.

We emerge from the tunnel into a huge open dome, fish of all shapes, sizes, and colors surrounding us. A square bar is situated in the middle of the area, also made from glass. As we get closer, I squint at the flecks of gold flickering through the clear panels. "Are they goldfish?"

Tom simply nods, remaining silent as I take in the space around me. A mezzanine encircles the entire dome, sectioned into six parts hidden behind more heavy blue curtains. "What's up there?" I ask, gesturing with my chin.

"Private booths," he says, pride emanating from him as he strides toward a set of stairs.

I take in the view as we reach the top. The main floor is broken into three distinct areas. One for lounging, filled with couches, large floor cushions, and armchairs. The second seems to be for dining. And the third is more like an actual bar with high-top tables encircled by stools.

Tom opens the curtain, letting me through first then closing it behind him.

Just as I take a seat on a sleek, dark-purple sofa facing the ginormous tank we're sitting inside, a petite redhead appears with an antipasto tray in hand. She places it on the small table in front of the sofa before turning to Tom. "What would you like to drink tonight, sir?"

Tom eyes me, and I shrug, then he orders for both of us. "Two whiskeys, neat. And keep them coming."

She gives a slight dip of her chin then vanishes through the curtain again.

"So, what do you think?"

"It's incredible. I kind of wish I'd found it first. I'd have doubled your offer just so I could have it for myself."

He chuckles. "I know. Why do you think I didn't bring you here until the deal was done?"

"Bastard," I mutter.

Two hours and four whiskeys later, I'm feeling the call of nature. "Where are the restrooms? I didn't see any downstairs."

"I'll show you." Tom leads the way, back the way we came, then through another tunnel to a hallway that, surprisingly, is not full of fish. The walls are a stark white. Two black doors indicate the men's and ladies' bathrooms, and I disappear inside one.

I'm unzipping my fly when a couple of guys stumble in, chatting so loudly I couldn't ignore them if I wanted to. I stare at the tiled wall in front of me as they continue their conversation.

Guy one says, "Brent, I'm telling you, bro. That is the same chick out there. We dated two years ago for like four months, and she was into fish, and the sex was out-of-this-world good. Then, boom. After three months, it turned to shit."

Guy two responds, "You think 'cause her name was Hannah, and she liked fish, and the sex was awesome till it wasn't that it's the same chick? That's the dumbest shit I ever heard."

His slurred words have me glancing at him from the corner of my eye. He hiccups and sways on his feet, clearly drunk off his ass.

Guy one snorts. "No, it's not. It makes perfect sense. You told me the first three months were awesome, then one day, it just wasn't anymore."

"So?" Guy two hiccups again.

Guy one slurs his words as the conversation continues. "Let's go find 'er and I'll prove it."

At this point, I'm not even pretending not to listen while I wash my hands then lean back against the counter.

Guy two snorts. "It's not the same Hannah."

Guy one shakes his head vigorously. "It *is* the same one. There's no other explanation."

Finally, they notice me standing by the sinks. They're so tanked they can barely stay upright without the assistance of the urinal dividers.

The first guy frowns. "Are you listening to our private conversation, bro?"

"If it was a private conversation, I wouldn't be able to hear it from across the room," I state.

Guy two turns to look at me, dick still in hand. "Okay. What do you think then, Mr. Know-it-All?"

Crossing my arms over my chest, I smirk. "I think this Hannah has low standards if she was dating either of you two."

Guy one shakes his head and sways on his feet. "No, that's not what he meant. You believe me, right? It's the same chick. It must be, like, her M.O."

I shrug. "Could be."

Guy one glares at guy two. "I told you, fucker!" Then he punches him in the shoulder, and streams of piss splash across the floor and urinal dividers. They start yelling at each other, and I take that as my cue to leave.

I roll the drunken dickwads' conversation over in my head as I walk back to Tom's private booth. Sitting beside him, I ask, "Does a Hannah work here?"

He eyes me over the rim of his drink. "I don't know. I haven't met everyone yet. Mostly just the bar staff. But there's another dozen or so that handle the tanks and fish. Why?"

"I think I might have found the woman who will give me exactly what I want."

HANNAH

RED ALERT! RED ALERT!

Why did I stick around and grab a drink before heading home tonight? Oh, that's right, because Amy begged me to. Stupid Amy and her stupid ideas.

I duck behind a couple involved in an intense conversation and receive a nasty glare from the woman. "Sorry," I whisper but don't move away from them. "Dodging an ex," I say quietly before peeking over the man's shoulder to check if I really did see what I thought I saw. Yes, yes, I did.

Brent and a guy I dated a few years ago, Peter, sit at one of the tall tables just six feet from my hiding spot. How do they even know each other? Why is this happening to me? I'm very particular about not dating men from the same circles, so this never happens. So what the hell?

Sweat gathers on my nape and palms. I rub my hands over my purple skinny jeans then reach for my phone from my back pocket to text Amy.

ME: ABORT. Brent is here . . . AND Peter. I'm out.

My phone starts ringing before I can even slide it back in my pocket. I answer, whisper-hissing into it, "What?"

"Where are you? I'm at the bar. I don't see Brent. And who's Peter?" Amy asks way too casually.

The people I'm using for cover sidestep, leaving me out in the open. I panic and dive behind a couch in the lounge area to my left.

"Wait, I just saw you. You're on the ground, aren't you?"

"What? I was like Flash fast, dude. You couldn't have seen me," I snap.

I'm greeted by silence.

"Amy? You still there?"

"Hannah?" a male voice I unfortunately recognize very well comes from above me. I tip my head back, meeting Brent's blue eyes as he stands over me.

"Oh, hi, Brent. Fancy seeing you here," I chirp.

"What are you doing down there?" he asks then hiccups.

He's drunk. Thank God. I get to my feet then hold out my phone. "Dropped this."

Brent sways a little but braces himself with a hand on the couch. "Really? 'Cause it looked like you dive-bombed the floor." He smiles his big, adorable, boy-next-door smile.

"Hey, Brent! How's it going?" Amy appears, giving him a friendly shoulder bump as she comes to a stop beside him. She sniffs then scrunches her nose. "Why do you smell like you pissed yourself?"

His eyes widen, and he sways again. "What? No I don't."

"Umm, yeah ya do. You might wanna call it a night, big man." She shoots him a wink then steps toward me, holding out her elbow to me.

I don't waste a second, looping my arm through hers and striding away as fast as my Chucks will take me. "Thank you for saving me," I whisper and press a quick kiss to her cheek.

"Sometimes, I don't know what you'd do without me."

"Thank God I'll never have to find out." We grin at each other as we reach the dining area, and one of the hostesses, Breanna, leads us through the crowded tables.

"Did you hear the new owner is in tonight?" Breanna asks as we sit.

I scan the room automatically. We haven't met yet, so I don't know who exactly I'm looking for. All I know is he's some rich dude who knows nothing about marine ecology but obviously has a good nose for business, because this place is booming.

Breanna points to one of the partitioned-off private rooms on the mezzanine. "He's up there. God, he's dreamy. Like, hot, dirty dreams, not that flowers-and-rainbow shit."

I choke on my water. "Good to know." I chuckle.

"Anyway, Mira says he's here with his cousin, and hot damn, that guy is smokin' too. Those boys must come from good stock, 'cause they're tall, dark, and hella handsome." She bites her ruby-red bottom lip. "What I wouldn't do to be the meat in *that* sandwich."

My interest is officially piqued. Bree is very selective, and her standards are outrageously high, so these guys must really be something special.

Glancing at Amy, her gaze is fixed on the room Bree pointed out, then her head tilts to the side. She whimpers and her jaw slackens. I click my fingers in front of her face. "Ames, are you having a stroke?" Shit, what are the signs of stroke again? I run through my medical training.

Amy shakes her head, snapping out of her daze, and stares at me. "What are you talking about? I'm not having a damn stroke. Look!" she says, jerking her chin in the direction she was just stroking out in.

I shift my gaze, and it all makes sense. I'm feeling a little strokey myself now.

Two of the most gorgeous men I have ever laid eyes on are nearing the bottom of the stairs, and I think I'm drooling a little. I track their movement to the bar where the slightly shorter of the two summons the bartender, Mike, over and talks to him for a moment before Mike points. Right. At. Me.

CHAPTER THREE

HANNAH

HOLY CRAP ON A CRACKER. THEY'RE HEADING THIS way. Oh my God, they're heading this way.

Amy kicks my shin under the table. "What are you doing? Close your damn mouth and be cool!" she hisses.

But I can't. I can't be cool. In fact, I'm the complete opposite of cool right now. I'm boiling hot, and my heart is pounding out of my stupidly tight chest. Maybe *I'm* having a stroke?

Oh goodness. I mentally run through my BE FAST checklist. Balance? Nope, it left the building. Eyes? They are obviously not working correctly, because those guys are getting closer, and it looks like they're smiling. Face? I can't shut my gaping mouth, so yep, face isn't working. Arms? Ah, no. My fingers have locked so tight around my water glass I'm afraid it will shatter. Speech? Umm, no. I don't even want to attempt to speak. Time? It's definitely time to call 911. I'm having a stroke, no doubt about it.

"Good evening, ladies," a deep voice yanks me from my panic attack.

I swallow and lift my eyes to meet those of the taller man, the one who just spoke. I open my mouth to say something, anything, but nothing comes out, so I snap it closed again.

"You'll have to forgive Hannah; she's had a long day," Amy says with a flutter of her lashes in the direction of the too-hot-for-this-world men. "How can we help you, gentleman?"

The slightly shorter guy extends a hand to Amy. "It would seem I assumed incorrectly that being the owner of this establishment would guarantee me a table whenever I so desired. We noticed you ladies have two free places at your table and hoped you'd allow us to join you."

Amy kicks me in the shin again—much harder this time. It's going to bruise, damn it. But it does the trick, and somehow, I finally gather my wits enough to speak. "Umm, sure, Mr. English." I hold out a shaking hand. "I'm Hannah. I work with the animals. And this is my friend Amy."

A Cheshire-cat grin spreads across the taller guy's perfect face, and I don't know if I should be aroused or afraid. Truth be told, I'm a little of both. Then, he takes the seat beside me while my new boss takes the one beside Amy. She practically vibrates in her seat while I'm left doing an imitation of a stunned mullet.

"Are you sure you don't mind us joining you?" that deep voice croons from my side.

I side-eye him, too chicken to look him fully in the face lest I start drooling. "Sure, why?"

His big body turns in his seat as he rests his elbow on the edge of the table and places his chin in his palm. He stares at the side of my head; it's extremely unnerving. "Forgive me if I'm wrong, but you look tense. Am I making you uncomfortable?"

I swallow. *Imagine he's naked; it'll make it easier to talk to him.* I close my eyes, swing my face in his direction, and open them.

Nope, the naked thing is not working. My gaze flits over his features, taking in his deep-blue eyes; his straight nose; those perfect, full, pillowy lips; the sharp, defined angle of his jaw; and the shadow of stubble covering it. . . I'm a goner. This dude's face alone is enough to make me spontaneously combust.

"I'm Sam," he says softly. "It's a pleasure to meet you, Hannah."

My tongue snakes out to wet my dry lips. "Hi, Sam," I murmur. He must think I'm all kinds of special right now, because that's all I can say. Nothing else comes to mind. Not a damn word. Any other day and you can't shut me up, but now, when words would come in super handy, I've got nothing.

Sam's lips twitch in what I assume is amusement. At least, I hope that's what it is. It could be a signal to his cousin to get him the hell away from the weird, mute chick he's been stuck with.

When I remain silent, he speaks again. "You said you work here, with the fish?"

I nod.

His free arm curls around the back of my chair as he makes himself more comfortable, and I tense further. He either doesn't notice or pretends not to, continuing with his line of questions. "What exactly do you do with the fish?"

My body relaxes slightly. The water is my safe space, where I'm most comfortable. I swallow the nerves squeezing my throat closed and force myself to speak. "I'm an aquarist," I say, feeling the passion for my work smothering the last of my anxiety. Taking a steadying breath, I smile. "Which basically means I'm a jack-of-all-trades when it comes to the aquarium. I oversee the monitoring of the water quality to maintain the well-being of all the species we have on display. But the sharks are my main area of expertise."

He blinks once, very slowly. I frown, and he loosens the top two buttons of his dress shirt.

"You okay?" I ask.

Sam clears his throat. "Are you about to tell me they're not man-eating beasts intent on eating me?"

My frown morphs into a full-blown scowl. "They most certainly are not man-eating beasts. That's a common misconception furthered by ridiculous, unrealistic, unsubstantiated propaganda promoted by fake news and movies." Nothing sets me off like people insulting my sweet babies.

He pops a brow. "The many people who have been eaten by them would beg to differ."

I jab a finger into his firm, muscled—*oh, dear God, so muscled*—chest. "Listen here, mister. You are more likely to be killed by a damn cow than a shark. Now, that's a fact you can take to the bank." I totally read that on one of my tampon packages, but it's legit.

"A cow? Really?"

"Yes, a cow. You want to point a finger at a vicious beast, there's your culprit," I tell him, crossing my arms. "My sweet girls wouldn't eat you if I sliced you open and threw you in their tank."

Those deep-blue eyes of his widen, then he chuckles. "Remind me never to go swimming with you."

Then, I realize the ridiculousness of what I just said. Because honestly, they probably would at least have a nibble if I did that. "I might get a little"—I hold my fingers up half an inch apart between us—"defensive of my babies."

"Noted," he murmurs, keeping his eyes fixed on mine. And the smile gracing his gorgeous face knocks the breath right out of my lungs.

SAM

THIS WOMAN IS A BREATH OF FRESH AIR. I'VE NEVER IN my thirty years met anyone like her. I can't stop smiling, and it's a genuine smile too. It feels amazing.

The weight that had settled on my shoulders after my run-in with Camille vanished the moment I laid eyes on the petite, pink-haired bombshell sitting next to me. And now that I've finally gotten her talking, I can't shake the feeling that she's going to turn my life upside down. And I'm totally on board with that.

When those guys were talking about a woman who, essentially, initiates splitsville with shitty sex after three months, I was determined to find her. But I'm having trouble reconciling the woman in front of me with the one they were talking about. I just can't see it.

"You look like you're thinking really hard right now. I promise I'm not going to try feeding you to my sharks," she says, a coy smile playing on her lips.

I want to kiss it right off her face, but I'm getting ahead of myself. I need to convince her to go out with me first. A few tendrils of hair brush against the back of the hand I have curled around her chair, and I turn my palm, catching a few in the tips of my fingers. Soft as silk and slightly damp.

"Were you working with your babies tonight?" I ask.

Hannah nods. "I got off my shift an hour ago."

"Do you swim with them? The sharks?"

She smiles so big her pearly white teeth peek out. "I do."

My skin prickles at the idea of getting in that tank, surrounded by . . . I swallow. My eyes flick to the aquarium to the left of us and spot a different shark than the one that swam over my head earlier. This one is much larger. "How many sharks are in there?" I gesture to the ceiling with my chin.

"Four." She says this like it's not a big fucking deal.

"You willingly swim in a tank with not one, but four sharks." I scan her small frame then return my gaze to her face. The amusement shining in her eyes gives me pause. "What?"

"You're scared of sharks, aren't you."

She doesn't pose it as a question, but a statement. I may as well have thrown my man card on the table and just let her have it, because she obviously has bigger balls than I do. "I prefer to think of it as having a strong sense of self-preservation."

Her laugh is light and melodic, and it hits me right in the gut.

"Right, whatever you say," she says, continuing to chuckle softly.

Being laughed at is not something I'm accustomed to. But surprisingly, I don't even care as long as I get to hear that sound.

A waiter appears to take our orders, and I'm stunned by the amount of food Hannah requests. The look on my face must betray my surprise.

"What, you thought I'd order a salad? Do I look

like I eat salad?" she asks, waving her hand over her tiny body.

"Umm, yes?" I hedge, unsure what else to say. She really is tiny, especially compared to me. I don't know where all the food she asked for is going to go.

She shakes her head and laughs again. "I'm a fully-fledged meat-eater, just like my girls. You don't get an ass like this from eating salad."

My gaze instantly shoots down her body, but my view's impeded by the table. "I wouldn't know. I haven't seen it."

"You'll have to take my word for it, then." She smirks.

I'm irrationally disgruntled by the possibility of not feasting my eyes on that ass of hers. "I'd prefer to make that judgment for myself."

"I'm sure you would. But I've been on my feet all day. You will just have to wait to watch me walk away at the end of the night." Then she winks.

When I first sat by her, I'd thought maybe she was being weird because she'd realized who I was and how much I'm worth. It wouldn't have been the first time a woman has freaked out at the prospect of my wealth. But then, when she relaxed and started talking about her job and joking with me, I realized it had nothing to do with money. She was simply nervous.

She treats me like I'm a normal, average guy. It's a novel feeling. *Does she know who I am and doesn't care, or is she completely clueless as to who she threatened to knife in a shark tank?* I'm tempted to ask, but I don't want to ruin this if it turns out she's none the wiser. So, I keep my thoughts to myself, instead, continuing with our flirtatious banter.

Leaning closer to her, I whisper in her ear, "What if I don't want you to walk away, Hannah?"

CHAPTER FOUR

HANNAH

Holy hot flushes. Is it warm in here? Yep, I'm pretty sure the air conditioner just broke down because I. Am. Dying.

Sam slowly leans back into his own seat, and I'm burning up like it's the hottest day on record since 1913. I snatch a napkin off the table and fan myself with it.

I must look like I'm going through *the change,* because Amy asks, "You okay, Han? You look a bit flushed."

It's the first thing she's said to me since Sam and Mr. English sat with us. I don't even know my new boss's first name because I've been so wrapped up in the man beside me.

"Yep, just dandy." It's a big fat lie, but I smile through it.

Amy gives me a knowing smirk. I narrow my eyes at her, silently telling her to keep her damn mouth shut. She turns her attention back to Mr. English. Sam remains silent at my side, and I glance at him from the corner of my eye to see a pleased expression on his face. I'd be pretty damn proud of myself, too, if I could turn a person to mush with only one sentence.

My heart is pounding so hard I'm sure everyone can see it trying to make a break for it right out of my goddamn chest. I place my hand over it and take a deep, calming breath and count to ten.

Just as I'm getting it back under control, tingles erupt over my skin as the soft pads of Sam's fingertips graze the skin of my nape. I whip my head to him and glare the best I can as he continues to torture me with his gentle caress.

"Stop that," I whisper-hiss.

He raises a brow. "You don't like it?"

"I didn't say that." I lick my lips. "What are you trying to do?"

A wicked grin tugs at his delectable mouth, and I can't drag my gaze away from it. "I'm making sure you'll give me your number at the end of the night . . . if nothing else."

Oh, he's good. Real good. I can't stop the smile that spreads across my face at his words.

We've got some intense chemistry going on, but I

am not easy. I don't do one-night stands, and if he thinks that is where this is heading, I've got news for him.

I reach around behind myself and remove his arm from the back of my chair. "As appealing as the idea of giving you more than my number is, it won't be happening. I'm just not that kind of girl, Sam." I flutter my lashes with mock innocence as I release his arm.

"And what kind of girl are you, Hannah?"

"Why, I'm the very best kind." I grin. "I'm fun."

His smile matches my own. "Oh, I bet you are. And wouldn't you know, a little fun is exactly what I've been looking for."

This guy. I want to fan myself again but refrain.

The waiter appears with our meals, and my mouth waters. I do love a good steak, and this one looks and smells amazing. After picking up my utensils, I cut a piece and pop it in my mouth, groaning as the tender meat melts on my tongue.

Sam nudges me with his elbow. "I never thought I'd be jealous of a steak, but as I live and breathe."

I chuckle. "Nothing beats a good steak. Absolutely nothing."

"I beg to differ." He snorts.

Shrugging, I place another piece in my mouth.

"Maybe you've never had a good steak. I'd offer you a bite, but I don't share my food."

"And maybe you've never had a good f—" He stops himself then clears his throat. "What I mean to say is, there are lots of other things more enjoyable than steak."

I throw my head back, laughing. "Nice save there, Sammy boy. Nice save."

He just shakes his head and cuts into the chicken breast on his plate. "I was trying to be a gentleman," he grumbles only loud enough for me to hear.

I slip one of the personal information cards I use at marine ecology conferences out of my bag and slide it across the table, leaving it next to his plate. "And I appreciate that very much," I whisper then go back to my delicious meal.

THE NEXT MORNING, I'M IMPERSONATING A SEA SLUG IN its natural state. That is, I'm lounging around my apartment in my underwear when my phone chimes with a text from none other than Sam.

My heart pitter-patters a little faster at the sight of his name.

SAM: I don't subscribe to the 'wait three days to make contact' rule. It's stupid and counterproductive. When can I see you again?

I chew my bottom lip as I contemplate my answer before my fingers fly across the screen.

ME: I agree. Life's too short to waste a whole three days. How about tomorrow?

SAM: How about today?

I blink at the screen. Damn, he's keen.

ME: Can you say eager beaver? I'm busy today.

SAM: So am I. But I can make time if you can.

Saturdays are my day of rest; it's a rule I never break. It helps keep a little distance between me and whatever guy I'm seeing at the time. I'm never available on a Saturday—ever. Avoiding meeting their families is also a must. It makes things smoother, allowing for a clean break when our time is up.

SAM: Hannah . . .

ME: I'm thinking.

SAM: What's there to think about? Come have breakfast with me, then you can do whatever it is you had planned.

I frown. *What is the time anyway?* Glancing at the clock on my phone, I'm not surprised it's only five-thirty. I'm physically unable to sleep in, but what's Sam's excuse for being awake at this hour?

ME ~Why are you awake this early on a Saturday?~

SAM ~Meet me for breakfast and I'll tell you.~

I shouldn't. It's not a good idea. I have these rules for a reason. *I am kinda hungry though . . .*

But no. I can't.

ME: Sorry, no can do.

SAM: Why not?

ME: Told you. I'm busy.

SAM: What could you possibly be doing at 5:30 in the morning?

Well, shit. What am I supposed to tell him? I can't say I have to work—all it would take is him asking his cousin and I'd be found out. I gnaw the corner of my bottom lip. The poor thing is getting a workout this morning. Aha! I'll throw Amy under the bus. He'll be none the wiser.

ME: I've got plans with Amy.

SAM: Oh, really? Because I just walked into Tom's place, and I'm pretty sure this is the shirt she was wearing last night... *Picture Attached*

I stare at the picture of a black-and-red polka dot T-shirt hanging off the tip of Sam's finger. Tom, aka Mr. English, offered to walk Amy back to her car last night when we left the bar. That dirty little tramp got busy with my boss, and now I've been caught out in my lie. But I'm already committed to it, so I push forward.

ME: That could be anyone's . . .

SAM

I run a frustrated hand through my shower-damp hair. I didn't expect Hannah to reply to my message until later this morning. Not many people are up as early as me, especially on the weekend. I was pleasantly surprised when she replied straight away, and I figured why not ask her out right now.

Her refusal to give me a reason for declining breakfast is driving me nuts. Any other woman would be all over the chance to share a meal with me. But apparently, not Hannah. I drop her friend's shirt on Tom's kitchen counter and text her back.

ME: We both know it's Amy's. Come have breakfast with me. I'm starving.

HANNAH: I can't.

Snatching the milk out of Tom's fridge, I stalk back across the hall to my place. We share the penthouse floor of the apartment building our grandfather gifted us for our twenty-fifth birthdays.

I drop the milk on the counter while I reply to Hannah.

ME: So you keep saying. But you still haven't given me a valid reason.

I'm being pushy. I know it, and I don't care. I decided last night that I want her, and damn it, I'm going to have her. I finish making my coffee while I wait for her response.

HANNAH: Because I said so, Sam. Just leave it at that. I'd be happy to have breakfast with you tomorrow, but today is not a possibility.

My teeth grind. Tomorrow. I can wait until then. I just don't want to.

ME: Fine. I'll pick you up. What's your address?

HANNAH: Bahahaha. I'm not telling you where I live! You could be a psycho with a fetish for rummaging through other people's trash. I'll meet you.

I blink. Then I blink again. Did she. . . I stare at

the screen, and despite myself, I laugh. Nobody has ever said anything like that to me before.

ME: I assure you I have not, and will never, rummage through trash.

HANNAH: Meh. There's a first time for everything.

Settling onto one of the stools in the kitchen, I sip my coffee.

ME: True. But not in this instance. Can I at least send a car for you?

HANNAH: Nope. Just tell me where to go. I can find my own way.

ME: Stubborn woman.

HANNAH: Stubborn, but fun ;)

I shake my head then send her the address of my building and tell her to be there by six. She might not want me to know where she lives, but I couldn't care less if she's aware of where I live. The restaurant downstairs will do just fine for our breakfast date.

Taking my coffee to my room with me, I stride into my closet and dress for another day in the office. Technically, I don't need to go in, but I have issues letting go of control. I can't help it. The need to see for myself that everything is as it should be is a compulsion.

On more than one occasion, I've been accused of being a workaholic, but the truth is, I simply haven't found anything I'd rather be doing. So, I work. I continue to build the family portfolio with new and interesting ventures that attract my attention and pique my curiosity.

I leave things like taking the family jet on spontaneous trips to Europe or sailing the yacht around the Bahamas for a month to Tom. That's more his style, although he does work hard when he's in the office.

He's suggested it's time I took a leaf out of his book and learned to relax. But honestly, if I were to take time off, I'd be bored out of my brain or stressing about how things were being run while I was away.

I reach for a white undershirt and slip it over my head before tugging a button-down from a hanger and sliding my arms in. As I take another swig of coffee, my mind goes back to Hannah. Behind my closed lids, I can see her gorgeous face and that pink hair of hers. A smile curves my mouth.

She is so damn pretty. I was instantly attracted to her last night, which caught me off guard—bright, outrageous hair doesn't generally do it for me. But it only served to make the aqua blue of her eyes stand out more.

Shaking myself out of my thoughts, I take a pair of jeans from the shelf and put them on. Drinking the last of my coffee, I give myself a quick once-over in the mirror and run my hand over the stubble coating my jaw. Normally, I'd shave before going into the office, but I have a feeling Hannah will like it, so I leave it and head out for the day.

Tomorrow can't come soon enough.

CHAPTER FIVE

HANNAH

WHAT DOES ONE WEAR ON A BREAKFAST DATE?

I searched the address Sam sent me, and it looks like we're eating at a fancy restaurant located on the ground floor of one of the most prestigious apartment buildings in the city. Tapping my finger on my chin, I peruse my closet in search of an appropriate outfit.

What could be fancier than glitter?! I snatch my glittery black capris from their hanger and pair them with a gorgeous crisp white, long-sleeve, silk blouse I've been dying to wear. It's still cool enough in the mornings to get away with long sleeves, thank goodness.

Now for shoes. I go back to tapping my chin as I run my gaze over my extensive shoe collection. Ha! My Jimmy Choo knock-offs will go beautifully with my outfit. Grabbing them from their perch, I check the time: five-twenty. Crap. I lay everything on the end of my bed then jump in the shower and clean myself off quickly.

Luckily, I washed my hair last night, so all I need to do is throw it in a quick braid that hangs over my shoulder.

When my hair is as good as it's going to get, I apply a light coat of foundation, some mascara, and gloss.

I order an Uber then throw on my clothes before giving myself a quick survey in my bedroom mirror. Not too bad, if I do say so myself. Another quick look at the time tells me I've only got ten minutes to make the twenty-minute trip. I forego waiting for the elevator and dash down the three flights of stairs to the lobby. Pushing through the front door, I'm pleased my ride is already waiting.

Sliding into the back seat, I smile at my driver. "Morning!"

She gives me a slight chin lift in acknowledgment, but that's all I get. She's obviously not a morning person, so I don't bother trying to fill the silence that permeates the car. Nervous energy surges through me when my phone chimes with a text from Sam.

SAM: I'm trying to decide if I'm being stood up or you're just running late.

Crap. He's obviously one of those people who are never late. And I'm the complete opposite. It doesn't matter how much time I give myself to get ready, I'm never on time. Except for work.

ME: Sorry. I'm on my way . . .

SAM: Good. I'll wait for you out front.

My knee bounces as the next five minutes drag by incredibly slowly. And then we arrive, and I'm out of the car with a hurried, "Thanks," to my driver as I slam the door.

Sam's dressed in a pair of dark-wash jeans and a white V-neck T-shirt. I admire the fact that the slight stubble that coated his jaw the other night is now thicker as he stands outside the most luxurious apartment complex I've ever seen. And somehow, he's even more devastatingly handsome in the daylight.

My heart rate spikes when I take him in, a dreamy little sigh slipping past my lips.

His eyes light as they rake over me from head to toe. "Wow, you look gorgeous."

I blush. I know I wasn't beaten with the ugly stick as a child, but hearing Sam say those words warms my insides. "Thank you," I murmur as I take his offered elbow and he leads me inside.

We're shown straight to a secluded table in the back, and I give Sam the eye. "Did you book this table before I arrived?"

"This is *my* table. I have breakfast here almost daily."

Rolling my eyes, I chuckle. "What, like you *own* this table? What if someone else was seated here before you arrived? Would you make them move?"

An impish grin pulls his delicious lips to the side. "Actually, I own Zenith. Well, Tom and I do. And nobody else sits here but myself or Tom."

I blink at him dumbly. *Did he just say he owns this building?* I take in our surroundings with new eyes. Holy. Shit.

"Now would be a great time for you to say something," Sam says, nudging me with his foot under the table.

What am I meant to say? I thought he'd picked this place for the food, not because he lives here. Let alone that he owns this whole damn building. What do I do with that?

"Hannah," he murmurs. "Is this okay? We can go somewhere else if you're uncomfortable."

Shifting in my seat, I lick my lips then look back to him. "I've made this awkward. I'm sorry."

He shakes his head. "No, I should have picked a different restaurant."

"This is fine, Sam—better than fine. I guess I wasn't expecting you to, well, own it."

"Is that a problem?" he asks, his vivid blue eyes searching mine.

Is it? Not really. It makes no difference to me if he has a bazillion dollars in his bank account. It's not like we're in this for the long haul. We'll hang out for a couple of months, have some fun, then go our separate ways—if it even goes that far.

Smiling at him, I say, "Not at all. I guess you caught me off guard. I wasn't expecting it, is all. Sorry for getting all weird on you."

He tilts his chin, his gaze assessing. "You sure?"

I smile wider and shimmy forward in my seat before leaning my elbows on the table. "Of course. So, what's good here? I'm starving."

And just like that, the air of awkwardness I

instigated evaporates, and we fall into comfortable small talk as we order our breakfast.

SAM

I CAN'T STOP STARING AT HER.

Hannah isn't like the other women I usually spend time with. For starters, her hair is pink and her pants are covered in glitter. I don't know much about fashion—okay, I don't know anything about fashion—but I do know that none of the women in my social circle would be caught dead in those pants or with that hair. It makes me like them even more.

I can't quite get over the way she speaks to me, either. In fact, I quite like it. Nobody else has ever refused to share a meal with me or threatened to feed me to a tank of sharks. She's light and airy; it's easy to be around her.

Even now, as she shovels her Eggs Benedict into her mouth like she's never eaten before, I can't take my eyes off her.

"What?" she asks. "Is there something on my face?"

All I can do is shake my head. "No, I just like watching you."

"Way to sound super creepy." She chuckles and wipes the corners of her mouth with a napkin.

"I can't say I've ever been accused of being creepy before."

Her eyes sparkle with humor. "I bet you say that to all the girls."

At this point, she has my mouth set in a permanent smile. "I can't reveal all my dirty secrets on our first official date."

Her brows arch, and a smirk curves her lips. "Is that what this is? A date?"

I nod. "What would you call it?"

She shrugs and takes a sip of her coffee. "I don't know. Two people getting to know each other."

"Otherwise known as a date," I supply.

"Potato—potawto. Doesn't really matter what we call it, does it?"

I relax in my chair, stretching my arms back then lacing my hands behind my head. "Not really. But I still don't know much about you, Hannah, except that you work at The Aquarium with the sharks. What else should I know?"

Hannah takes a moment before answering me. "There's not much to know, really. I'm an only child whose parents have sadly both passed away. I'm twenty-eight, career-focused, love starfish, hate toadfish, and I share an apartment with a lobster named Levi, short for Leviathan. He's quite the little charmer. You'll have to meet him sometime."

I cock a brow then shake my head. "I shouldn't be surprised, should I? I mean, you refer to sharks as sweet babies."

"I think I was a mermaid in a past life," she says on a dreamy sigh. "So, what about you? What do I need to know, Sam? Please include any weird sexual fetishes in your rundown—just so we can get those out of the way here and now. I reserve the right to veto anything too outrageous."

I cough. She's a riot. I'm enjoying this way too much to stop her, even though the waiter clearing our empty plates away has just turned fifty shades of red. "Weird sexual fetishes?" I sit forward, supporting my elbows on the table and cupping my jaw as if to think about her absurd question. "Nope, don't have any. Doesn't everyone collect their lovers' toenail clippings while they're sleeping?"

Hannah throws her head back and laughs. It's a beautiful sight, and it sounds as good as it did the other night.

When she's regained a semblance of control, I cock a brow. "What? You don't do that?"

She wipes a tear away from the corner of her eye, and I'm ridiculously pleased that I'm the one who produced this reaction from her. I'm not known for being an amusing person, but I couldn't help myself. She makes me want to be, just so I can listen to her laugh.

"Oh my God. Stop. You're too much." She gasps and I grin, pride blooming in my chest at my accomplishment.

CHAPTER SIX

HANNAH

THE OTHER TABLES IN ZENITH'S RESTAURANT ARE beginning to fill as Sam and I are leaving. Which reminds me . . . "You didn't tell me why you were up so early yesterday—or today, for that matter."

"I'm in the gym by five every morning. It's a habit I can't break nowadays."

I stop dead in my tracks. "That sounds awful."

Sam shakes his head at me and places a palm on my lower back, urging me onward. "You were awake when I messaged you yesterday. And you agreed to an early breakfast today, so obviously mornings don't bother you. What's so awful about it?"

"I'm not worried about early mornings—I can't sleep past five myself. It's the gym." I cringe. "No, thank you. Everybody's sweat mingling on the equipment. It's nasty."

He chuckles as we come to a stop outside *his*

building. "It's a great way to start the day, gets your blood pumping and creates endorphins. Win–win. Also, there are these things called sanitary wipes that the machinery is cleaned with after each use."

I pat his chest, patronizing him. "Okay, gym junkie, whatever you say. I'll stick to going for a dip with my girls. That wakes me plenty."

Sam grimaces. "I'd rather be a gym junkie than insane. Of course swimming with sharks wakes you up—your subconscious is preparing for an inevitable bloody death."

Oh. My. Goodness. This guy. I can't contain my laughter. "You're a hoot. But you know I've just made it my personal mission in life to get you in that tank with me one day," I say with a wink.

He blanches. "The hell you will."

I waggle my eyebrows as I walk backwards to my awaiting Uber. "We'll see," I say then slam the door on Sam's response, laughing at the expression on his face as the car pulls away from the curb.

Unsurprisingly, a text chimes on my phone before I've reached the end of the block.

SAM: It's not going to happen. Ever.

ME: I think it will.

SAM: I think you're deluding yourself.

ME: Is little Sammy scared of the big bad sharks?

SAM: Little Sammy feels as strongly about this as I do.

I snicker and my Uber driver eyes me through the rearview mirror as if I'm a crazy person. Ignoring him, I tap out my reply.

ME: Are you telling me you refer to your penis as Little Sammy?

SAM: What? No! I was just making my point.

ME: Sure you were. Anyway, I've decided it's my turn to pick where we go next since you chose today. When are you free?

SAM: Who's the eager beaver now?
SAM: I could do lunch on Tuesday.

ME: I'll be working. How about Thursday evening?

SAM: I can make that work. Where are we going?

I'm going to show him how us regular folk kick it.

ME: I'll send you the address in time for you to get there. But you can't Google it. It's a surprise.

SAM: I don't do surprises.

ME: You do now.

SAM

THURSDAY AFTERNOON ...

Tom and I have been reviewing the employment contracts all day for a company we recently acquired. The salaries the CEO and VP are collecting are insane compared to the profit margin of the company. It's no wonder it was going under.

After hours of reading, the words on the page are beginning to blur together, so I set them aside and text Hannah.

ME: So, where's this address?

HANNAH: It won't take long to get there. I'll send it when you need it. Be ready by seven.

God, this woman is going to drive me crazy. If I didn't know better, I'd think pushing my buttons was her new favorite pastime.

ME: Now is good.

HANNAH: So is seven.

ME: Hannah . . .

HANNAH: Patience is a virtue ;)

I loosen a frustrated growl and drop my phone on my desk with a thud. Patience may be a virtue, but it's never been one of mine.

"What's got your panties in a bunch?" Tom asks from the other side of my desk.

"Hannah is doing my head in."

Tom smirks. "Already? Maybe you should hand her over to me. I'm sure I can handle her."

I scowl. "Fuck off, dickwad. You're not going anywhere near her. Besides, didn't you hook up with her friend?"

"That I did. And I'm seeing her again tomorrow," he says with a shit-eating grin. "Having trouble sealing the deal, cousin?"

"You're an asshole, you know that?" But I'm aware he's just being a wise-ass. I crack my knuckles then strum my fingers on the edge of my desk. "She's different, Tommy. I've never met anyone like her."

He scoffs. "Of course not. You think the women at the country club would get in a fish tank full of sharks?"

I shake my head. "It's not only the shark thing— although, that is a big part of it. It's everything. The way she talks to me, how she dresses, her laugh. I actually *want* to spend time with her."

My cousin simply nods. He knows exactly what I'm talking about. We have the same issue when it comes to women.

After Hannah got over the initial shock of me telling her I own Zenith, she was back to making jokes at my expense and eating like there was no tomorrow. Not a flicker of wedding-bell scheming to be seen.

"So what's the problem?" Tom asks.

"I don't know what to do with her. Like tonight, we're meant to be going out, but she won't tell me where. She's going to send me the address when it's time to leave. Who does that?" I throw my arms out, exasperated.

Tom laughs. "I like it. She's keeping you on your toes. Just go with it, Sam. It's not going to kill you to hand over control for one night."

"It's not about control," I huff.

He rolls his eyes at me. "Yes, it is. You can't handle someone else holding the reins. Sit back and enjoy the ride, man."

Tom's always been the free spirit of the two of us. I don't know how he does it, but if I'm going to keep seeing Hannah, I guess I'm going to have to learn.

HANNAH

I SENT SAM THE ADDRESS TO MOJO'S BOWLING ALLEY ten minutes ago. He didn't reply.

We may have only spent time together twice, but it was enough for me to get a good read on him. He lives the upper-class, silver-spoon life. I'd bet my life savings he's never been to a place like this.

That thought makes me irrationally happy. I'm

so excited to see how he reacts to being pushed out of his comfort zone.

I'm leaning against the outside wall, under the flashing neon sign, when a sleek black town car pulls up. I grin when Sam steps out, frowning at the establishment I've chosen for our night together.

I push off the wall and stride over, but not before I glare at the group of women practically drooling on themselves at the sight of him. "Hey there," I say, my eyes roving up and down his tall frame. *God, he's a fine specimen.* Just looking at him has my bits tingling in awareness.

He raises a brow at me when I come to a stop before him. His gaze rakes over my body, sending chills skating across my skin at the hunger clear in his eyes. I swallow—hard. "Hey," I mumble again.

"Hey," he says in a husky tone that has my toes curling. Then, he steps forward, closing the gap I'd left between our bodies. His large palm snakes around my waist, settling in the center of my back as he tugs me into his warm chest then drops his mouth to my ear. "I think you're trying to kill me, Hannah," he murmurs.

My hands shoot out, gripping his firm biceps to steady myself. "Why would you think that?" I ask, my voice shaky.

"You're more beautiful every time I see you. It makes things very *hard* for me," he growls, rolling his hips into my lower belly.

My knees quake, and heat pools in my lady parts. Holy smoked salmon. He is hard—like, really hard. I almost say, *'To hell with bowling—let's bone instead!'* because God, he feels good. His palms skate along my spine, going lower each time.

I turn my face, my lips lightly grazing his cheek as I force words out. "We should go inside."

Sam rolls his hips again. "We should get in my car," he counters.

It's an enticing offer, and I'm so damn tempted. I squeeze my eyes shut, trying to gain control over my raging libido. We're supposed to be bowling, not banging. It's a struggle to remind myself of my three-date rule when he's this close.

Mustering all my resolve, I step out of his hold. I slide my hands over his corded arms as I go until our fingers are our only point of contact. "Come on, horndog. Bowling first. Then we'll see where the night takes us." I wink and tug him toward the entry.

He releases one of my hands. "Fine, just give me a sec," he grumbles then reaches to rearrange his package.

I can't take my eyes off his hand as he repositions

his boner. *I gave him that. And I didn't even have to touch it!* My smile is so wide it hurts my cheeks.

CHAPTER SEVEN

SAM

I COULD HAVE SWALLOWED MY TONGUE AT THE SIGHT of her waiting outside in that little black top and red tartan skirt showing a sliver of her creamy stomach. My dick thought all his Christmases had come at once.

I've had to adjust my junk every damn time she's bent over to roll the ball down the lane. She's not flashing the whole place or anything, since she's got black tights covering her legs and hiding all the good stuff under that skirt. But damn, the visual of bending her over my couch in nothing but that skirt and those chunky boots . . .

Hannah strides back to where I'm sitting behind the dingy scoreboard. "Did you get that?" she asks when she notices I haven't entered her most recent tally.

I blink at her. "Nope. I was distracted by the view."

Her grin is breathtaking as she leans in and plants a kiss on my jaw. "I've been a bit distracted myself," she croons in my ear, then—*Lord, save my soul*—she nips the lobe.

"Hannah," I growl, tugging her down into my lap, unable to go on without touching her again. I shift my hips, letting her feel exactly how uncomfortable this evening is for me. She wiggles, and I have to squeeze her thighs to keep her still. "I'm going to kiss you now, and you're going to let me," I tell her before slamming my mouth onto hers.

It's not gentle or soft. I devour her lips, sliding my tongue along the seam, forcing her to open for me. My fingers dig into her hips when she moans into the kiss, her tongue tangling with mine. I break away, my hard-on now throbbing painfully beneath her pert little ass.

"If you're done torturing me," I hiss into her mouth, "I think it's time to leave."

Her answering nod is the only confirmation I need. I stand and Hannah's lithe form slides down my front. Looping my hands around her waist, I bend to kiss her again. She melts into me, and damn, if that doesn't feel good—the power I have over her body.

"My place or yours?" I ask.

"Mine's closer," she breathes.

Suits me fine. I take her hand and lead her to the exit, following her when we reach the street and she tugs me along the sidewalk.

"Three blocks this way," she says, speeding up once we're past a group of people lingering in front of the bowling alley.

My fingers flex around her hand, loving her impatience as she curses under her breath at the 'Do Not Walk' symbol we're stopped at. Her booted foot taps rapidly against the pavement, then she's off, yanking me along behind her the second we're able to safely cross.

Not ten minutes later, we arrive at her apartment building. I don't even have time to take in the façade as Hannah ushers us through the doors and into the foyer.

"Evening, Steve." She waves to an elderly gentleman sitting in a lounge reading a newspaper, a small fluffy dog sitting in his lap, as we wait for the elevator. The dog barks at her, wiggling its tail in excitement, and she smiles impossibly wide. "Hey, Ginger," she croons, and the dog yaps back again.

Steve eyes me over the top of his newspaper. "Evening, Miss Archer," he says then adds, "and friend."

I dip my chin. "Good evening, sir."

"Eyes off, Steve," Hannah chastises, and the way he's looking at me suddenly makes sense.

The elevator doors slide open, and Steve's chuckle follows behind us as we step inside. The second they close, I have Hannah pinned, my mouth on the sweet skin of her throat. Her fingers tangle in my hair, but we arrive on her floor before I can do anything more.

I grip her hips from behind, rolling mine into her ass as she jams her key in the lock and throws the door to her apartment open. She spins in my arms when we step over the threshold, backing me against the wall then yanking me to her by my collar to kiss the shit out of me.

Her fingers fumble with the buttons of my shirt until she lets out a frustrated little growl and tugs at either side, sending buttons flying. I scoop her up by her thighs, reversing our position as I pin her with my hips, and her legs curl around my waist.

I'm desperate to be inside her, but I need to see her first. My hands slide under the hem of her top, pushing it past her ribs and above her breasts. Our mouths part only long enough for me to pull it over her head and discard it on the floor.

Hannah's hands latch onto the buckle of my belt,

unfastening it then my jeans. Her little hand skates across my happy trail under the band of my boxer briefs until she's gripping my cock in her warm palm. My hips surge forward, and my neck strains at the sensation that shoots down my spine.

"Bedroom," I grunt into her mouth with another thrust of my hips.

"Second door on the right."

Digging my hands into her ass cheeks, I stride down the short hallway before dropping her onto the bed in the center of the room. She jackknifes, arms going behind her back to unfasten her bra while I kick my pants off to the side then let my ruined shirt fall to the ground.

Leaning over her, I take one of her rosy nipples into my mouth before sucking gently as I pinch the other—hard. Her torso arches, pushing her chest into my face. My free hand finds its way under her skirt and hooks in the band of her tights. I tug them and her underwear downwards.

I want her just like this: wearing this skirt, these boots, and nothing else. Her tights pool around her ankles, and I release her breasts to drag her to the edge of the bed.

Her eyes eat me up, roving over my body with liquid heat. She reaches forward and trails a finger down the center of my chest, all the way to the band of my boxers. She flattens her palm over my straining cock before dropping her lips to lightly suck the head through the thin layer of fabric.

"Fuck, Hannah," I groan.

When she glances at me, the feral need shining in her gaze has me removing my boxers in a flash and reaching for my wallet in my pants. After retrieving the condom, I drop my wallet back to the floor then sheath my cock in the latex. Hannah watches my every move, a seductive smirk on her pretty lips and fuck if it doesn't make me harder.

Leaning in, I grab hold of her hips and flip her so she's bent over the side of the bed, her ass in the air, waiting for me to slap it. I've never spanked a woman before, but the urge rises in me so powerfully I do it without a second thought. Hannah squeals but pushes back into my awaiting cock, her slick pussy begging for me.

Grabbing her cheeks, I drop to my knees and run my tongue through her soaked folds. She tastes of woman and sex. The sounds she makes move me back to my feet. I lean over her, taking my cock with one hand and guiding it to her entrance before surging forward.

"Ahh, Sam . . . yes!" she cries out, and I can't stay still. I have to move; I have to fuck.

My thrusts are hard and deep. Hannah quivers beneath me, whimpering with every glide in and out. Reaching a hand under her, I find her clit and run tiny circles around it, never quite touching it where she needs it most. Her body begins to quiver, and I pound into her harder, faster.

"Come for me, baby," I command, sinking my teeth into her shoulder at the same time as I finally pinch her clit between my fingers.

Her moan ricochets off the walls as her body clenches around my cock so hard I shoot my load. I slow my movements then still inside her. My head spins with the intensity of my release, and I slide out of her warmth before dropping to lie beside her.

We stay like that, panting and staring at each other, for a good few minutes as we come down from the high of amazing sex.

"Better than steak?" I murmur, grinning when her eyes light with amusement.

A small chuckle escapes her. "So much better."

CHAPTER EIGHT

HANNAH

THAT WAS, BY FAR, THE HOTTEST FIRST-TIME-WITH-A-partner sex ever. Zero awkwardness, no *"Is this okay?"*, and a mind-numbing orgasm, to boot.

My legs feel like jelly, and I'm beyond satisfied. I want to curl up and have a quick power nap.

But as reality sets in, it dawns on me: I threw my three-dates rule out the window.

"You okay?" Sam asks, stroking my back with gentle fingers.

I swallow then nod. *It's okay. It was just one little rule. No big deal, right?*

Sam's hand stills on my shoulder. "Hannah, did I do something wrong?"

Licking my lips, I run my gaze over his concerned face. "I have a three-date rule. I don't like to sleep with someone until we've been out at least three times, and I—" I sit, tugging the blanket with me and wrapping it around my mostly naked body.

My legs tangle in my tights still wrapped around my ankles, and I kick and thrash, trying to dislodge them.

"Hey," Sam says, taking my legs in his hands. "Let me help." He tugs off my boots, dropping them on the floor with a thud, then removes my tights.

"Thank you," I murmur, embarrassed by my little spack-out. Tucking my legs beneath me, I lift my eyes to Sam's ridiculously handsome face. "Sorry. I'm not usually weird after sex."

His brows furrow as he stares at me with so much intensity I have to look away.

A warm palm cups my jaw, turning my face to look at him. "I'm sorry for coming on so strong tonight. I had every intention of being a gentleman —that is, until my eyes landed on you." A gentle smile curves his lips. "Everything about you throws me off center. And when I saw you tonight . . . the drive to claim every single part of you took over, and it was all I could think about."

Well, when he says that, how can I be upset about it?

I lift my hand and place it over his, still holding my jaw so gently. Such a contradiction to the amazing sex we just had. "I'm not blaming you. I just have these rules, and they help me keep things straight in my head. I overreacted. It's not a big deal that we rounded all the bases a little earlier than I expected. I'm definitely not complaining." I grin, hoping like hell he understands.

Sam nods, and his thumb strokes my bottom lip. "If it makes you feel any better, we can count the night we met as our first date. That makes tonight date number three."

My cheeks pull tight as my smile spreads across my face. Then, I throw the blanket to the side and launch myself at him. He falls back, and I end up straddling his incredible body. I run my greedy hands across his sculpted chest, marveling at every rise and fall of his muscles.

"You'd better stop touching me unless you're ready for round two," Sam warns me with an upward thrust of his hips. His dick glides against my butt, and I spin around. *He's getting hard again.*

"Already?" I ask, shocked and delighted.

The grin that crosses his lips is downright wicked. "Apparently so."

I scurry off of him and reach for the spent condom still covering his length. Discarding it in a tissue from my side table, I open the top drawer and grab a fresh one. Sam's eyes follow me as I tear the package open, remove the condom, then toss the packet over my shoulder. He chuckles then chokes on the sound as I wrap my hand around his thick dick and roll the rubber to his base.

THE BUZZING OF MY ALARM WAKES ME FROM A DEEP sleep. I slap my hand around until it lands on it, and I turn it off. I'm usually up before it even has a chance to go off, but not after last night. It's official: Sam is a very talented lover with unbelievable stamina.

I'm not sure what time it was when he pressed his lips to my shoulder and murmured his goodbyes. I was so exhausted I think I was asleep before he was even out of my apartment.

Rolling out of bed, I snatch my phone and stumble to the bathroom. Dropping onto the toilet, I read a text from Sam as I relieve myself.

SAM: I'm ready for date number four when you are. But this one's on my terms.

Warmth fills my chest, and I set my phone aside and get in the shower. My body is sore, but in a you-had-incredible-sex-several-times-last-night kind of way.

I'm still smiling when I arrive at work an hour later. I'm in such a good mood I don't even care that the food-preppers are down a man, thus my girls' breakfast is running late. I've never been one to sit still, so I start loading what has been prepared with my babies' vitamins.

"You're awfully chipper this morning," Tami, one of the preppers, says, nudging me in the ribs with her elbow.

I waggle my brows back at her. "I've had four very good reasons to plaster this smile on my face recently."

She bursts out laughing. "Damn, girl. Where can I get me a man who delivers like that?!"

"I don't even know how I got him," I tell her, shrugging. And the statement rings true. *Why did Sam and Tom approach Amy and me in the first place?* I don't buy that Tom couldn't get a table, but I didn't even think to ask. And now it's bugging me.

I finish stuffing the last chunk of tuna with a horse-sized vitamin then go scrub my hands in the huge stainless-steel sink. After pulling my phone from my pocket, I send Sam a quick text, asking him about it.

ME: So, you never did tell me why you guys crashed Amy's and my girls' night...

Violet approaches as I slide my phone away. "Morning, Vi."

"Hey, Han. You busy? Wanna help me bring my guys in?"

"Sure." We have to move the turtles into a separate area when we feed the sharks since we use the same method to feed them. We don't want one of my girls getting a little overeager and taking a chunk out of one of Violet's turtles if they swim on over, thinking it's a snack for them.

Vi hands me one of the colored rods we use to signal the turtles, and we make our way to the top of the tank. It doesn't take Mate and Sheela long to spot their rods in the water and come over.

"Thanks. It's easier with two people. I'm on my own today. Leila's down with something," Vi says as she hands a cabbage leaf to Mate.

"Something must be going around. The preppers are out a man today, too. Anyway, let me know if you need a hand with anything else. I'm off to feed my babies."

It takes four people just to feed my girls, then another to operate the shoots that release food into the water at the bottom of the tank to keep the bottom feeders happy. Plus two more who scatter food at the opposite side from where my girls are fed to keep everyone else away.

Walking back into the prep room, I scoop up the bucket labeled *Tina*. "Let's go, people," I call, and everyone nods as we file out of the room, buckets and feeding poles in hand.

There's one feeder assigned to each shark. Tina is my main girl and the largest of our collection. She's a ten-foot tiger with a little bit of an attitude. Then there's Ruby, our blacktip reef shark; Lulu is a lemon shark; and Bertha is a bull. The girls have all been trained to feed from the same spot at the same time every feed.

My phone chimes in my pocket, and I pull it out. Sam has replied to my earlier text.

SAM: We were hungry and two beautiful women were eating alone. It made sense to ask if we could join you.

But that doesn't explain them talking to Mike at the bar and him clearly pointing at me from across the room before they headed our way.

ME: I totally saw the conversation you guys had with the bartender and him pointing at us. What was that about?

My phone rings in my hand before I can put it back in my pocket. It's Sam. "Hey," I answer.

He clears his throat. "What are you doing right now?"

"I'm about to feed a ten-foot tiger shark. You?"

I chuckle at his muttered curse before he replies, "Nothing so life-threatening. Are you free for lunch later? I think it's best if I explain the bartender situation in person."

My brows furrow. "As intrigued as I am now, I can't. We're short-staffed today."

"Okay, how about tomorrow?" he counters.

I nibble my bottom lip. I don't have time to talk right now; all the other feeders are waiting on me. "Crap, I've gotta go. I'll text you later, okay." I end the call before he responds.

"Sorry, guys, let's do this!" I say, forcing a smile I'm not quite feeling. Why does Sam need to explain in person? And why did he call it a situation? That makes it sound like it's a big deal. An unwelcome feeling settles in my gut.

CHAPTER NINE

SAM

SHE HUNG UP ON ME.

I stare at my phone in shock. This is another first for me.

Maybe I handled that wrong. Should I have acted like I didn't know what she was talking about when she asked about the bartender? I lean back in my chair and look out at the cityscape beyond the floor-to-ceiling window of my office.

Last night was amazing. We were amazing together. And if I've fucked that, I'll be royally pissed. But so far, I've been completely honest with Hannah, and I have no intention of lying to her now.

I don't think she'll be angry with my reason for seeking her out that night. From what the guys in the bathroom were saying, she should be right on board with what I want with her. We probably should have discussed it before last night happened, but it's not like I planned to fuck her brains out.

Before I can dwell on it all for too long, Tom throws the door to my office open and struts in wearing the most hideous suit I've ever seen. I burst out laughing. "What the hell are you wearing?"

He flips me off. "This beauty is from Bobby James's new exclusive line, thank you very much. It costs thirty-six thousand dollars," he says, running his hands over the lapels.

I roll my eyes. "Just because it's obscenely expensive does not mean it's worth it. That thing is" —I examine the eggplant-purple atrocity—"an eyesore."

"Jealousy doesn't suit you, Sammy. It's not my fault you lack the confidence to pull off a suit like this. Also, I simply pointed out how much it costs. I didn't say I paid for it. Bobby asked me to be the face of his new line."

"And you said yes? Was that before or after you saw it?" I ask, genuinely curious now.

Heaving a sigh, he drops into the chair across from me. "Before, but that's irrelevant."

It's after eight when I finally hear from Hannah.

HANNAH: Sorry for the late message. Work was crazy busy. This week isn't going to work out for me.

We've got a few people down with the stomach flu. I don't know when I'll be able to see you.

After last night, I'm hornier than a teenager. I don't want to wait a whole week before seeing her again. But she's already called me a creeper once, so I'm not going to tell her that.

ME: Okay. Next weekend then?

HANNAH: Sounds good. Let me know where and when.

I send her the address of my favorite restaurant, Alejandro's, then tell my secretary to make a reservation for next Saturday evening. I don't actually have any intention of waiting until then to see Hannah, though. If she can't get away from work, I'll go to her.

Now that I know she knows it was no accident that brought us together, I have an overwhelming urge to explain myself.

THREE DAYS LATER, I GOT TOM TO GIVE ME THE security codes to enter the restricted staff zones behind the scenes of The Aquarium. He didn't even ask why I wanted them; he simply gave me a knowing grin then handed them over.

After punching in the code on the digital lock at the staff entrance by the rear parking lot, I go in search of Hannah. A guy wearing a wetsuit steps in front of me, placing a hand on my shoulder, attempting to steer me back toward the exit. "You can't be back here, sir."

I dig in my heels, look at his hand, then pluck it off, dropping it away from me. "First, don't touch me. Second, I can go where I please, and third, where's Hannah?"

His forehead scrunches as he eyes me. "Who are you and what do you want with Hannah?"

A feminine voice comes from down the hall. "Sam? What are you doing here?"

I sidestep the guy and stride toward a similarly dressed Hannah. "Bought you lunch," I say, gesturing to the takeout I picked up on my way here. "You couldn't get away from work, but I could. So, here I am."

She frowns at the brown bag in my hand then leans toward it, sniffing. "What is it?"

"Medium rare eye fillet with garlic sauce and a side of fries."

Her eyes light, and she snatches the food from my outstretched hand. "Follow me," she says over her shoulder as she walks farther down the hallway.

She doesn't have to tell me twice. I'm on her heels, my eyes fixed on her ass swaying as she goes. It looks amazing wrapped in that skintight blue wetsuit. But I'm not the only one who notices. The guy who stopped me before is also watching her. I close the distance between us and curl a possessive hand around her small waist, walking beside her instead of behind her.

Hannah leads us to a room at the very end of the hall then closes the door behind me. I don't miss the click of the lock or the seductive little grin on her pretty mouth when she does it.

Glancing around, I take note of the two couches pushed against the wall and the table with long bench seats on either side. When I turn back to Hannah, my mouth goes dry. She's tugging down the zipper on the front of her wetsuit, slowly revealing more and more of her creamy flesh.

I swallow. "You don't want to eat your steak?"

All I get is a shake of her head, then she's on me. I trip backwards, landing on the couch behind me, and she quickly scrambles into my lap. Her lips press to the edge of my jaw, followed by a sweep of her tongue with a roll of her hips over my growing hard-on.

"Jesus, Hannah," I groan. I came here to feed her and talk. As horny as I've been, I didn't intend on fucking her at her place of work. But the way her hips keep rolling over me, that's exactly where this is going.

I grip her waist, holding her still. "We should talk. I wanted to—"

She cuts me off with a swipe of her tongue over my bottom lip. Christ. I tried. That counts for something, right?

Dragging one hand along her now naked spine, I tangle my fingers in her damp hair and tug her head back. She squirms in my lap when I lift my mouth to her slender throat and suck. A moan escapes her, and her hands yank at my belt then undo my fly.

I let go of her to dig my wallet out of my pocket. Hannah takes it from me, snatches the foil package out, then drops the leather to the couch beside us. I'm transfixed as she wraps one hand around my length and slides the condom down my shaft with the other.

She strokes me, once, twice, three times. Then I

lift her and swing, depositing her on her back on the couch. She helps me rip her wetsuit off, kicking it to the floor when it's free of her ankles.

She is so damn beautiful spread out beneath me like this: hair damp and splayed around her head like a halo, nipples hard and peaked, her chest rising and falling in rapid succession. I glide a hand down her throat, over her collarbone, between the valley of her breasts, and across her taut stomach.

"Sam, just fuck me already!" she demands, reaching for my cock and tugging it toward her entrance.

I steady myself with a hand beside her head, but refuse to enter her until I'm sure she's wet for me. "Wrap your legs around me, baby," I instruct. When she complies, I reach between us, run two fingers through her folds, then push them inside her slick heat.

Hannah squirms. "Please, Sam."

My cock jolts at her plea, and I remove my fingers, bring them to my mouth, and suck them clean before dropping to kiss her deeply, letting her taste herself on my tongue.

Shifting my hips, I align myself with her entrance and thrust hard and deep. I still for a moment, enjoying the feel of being inside her again.

She digs her heels into my ass. "Fuck me, Sam. Please fuck me. You feel so good," she whimpers, wriggling her hips beneath me.

"Such a dirty mouth," I croon, gliding my cock in and out in long, slow strokes. She squirms beneath me. "You want more, baby?"

She nods frantically.

"I'm going to need you to say it, Hannah. I like that dirty little mouth of yours." I continue to taunt her with excruciatingly slow glides in and out of her. It's killing me, too, but I want words.

She moans, her heels pressing relentlessly into my ass, trying to force me to go faster. "Please, Sam."

"Please what? What do you need, Hannah?"

A frustrated growl rips from her lips, her eyes blazing with fire as she says, "Fuck me hard and fast, Sam. Now!"

My lips quirk in what I'm sure is the most cocky grin I've ever worn. "As you wish," I whisper over her kiss-swollen lips. Then, I give her what she wants. I pull out almost all the way then slam back in hard and fast just like she's asked.

HANNAH

My day couldn't possibly get any better. Sam surprising me with not only lunch, but a steak lunch. And then the quickie on the couch . . . I am so blissed out right now.

Sam is refastening his black suit pants as I lie here taking him in. I'm too sated to move just yet.

"What?" he asks with a raised brow.

I give him a lazy smile. "Nothing. Can't a girl simply enjoy the view?"

He gives my thigh a playful smack. "Come on. Your steak will be getting cold."

"A good steak tastes good hot or cold. And I'm willing to bet you didn't bring me a subpar steak."

Sam shrugs then offers me his hand, and I take it before sitting with his assistance. He passes me my discarded wetsuit. "Have you got something else you could put on, or is this your uniform?"

"I was actually on my way back here to get changed when I saw you," I tell him as I walk naked to my locker then pop it open and grab a fresh pair of underwear and clothes.

I feel his eyes on me as I slide the black lace thong up my legs. Peeking over my shoulder, I give him a wicked grin.

He clears his throat. "You wear sexy lingerie every day, or are you trying to kill me?"

"Every day. There's something empowering about wearing sexy lingerie under regular clothes. It's like I have a secret that nobody else knows."

"Well, now I know. And I like it," he says, stepping into me from behind. "A lot." He takes the clasp of my bra from me and fastens it himself before gliding his hands along my naked sides.

I tip my head back, resting it against his shoulder as his hands trace light patterns over my skin. "That feels nice," I murmur.

"Good," he says in a husky whisper. "Because I'm going to be touching you every chance I get." Then his lips press to mine, gentle and sweet.

A few minutes later, we're sitting at the break-room table when I ask Sam, "So, what did you want to talk about?"

He wipes his mouth with a napkin then clears his throat. "Well, you asked why Tom and I talked to the bartender before approaching you and Amy that night. The truth is . . ." He strums his fingertips on the table and looks away for a moment.

"Sam, whatever it is, I'm sure it's fine. Just say it, 'cause you're making me nervous."

His eyes immediately dart back to mine. "Sorry. You're probably right. At least, I hope you are."

That sentence does not soothe my nerves at all.

CHAPTER TEN

HANNAH

I STARE AT SAM, WAITING FOR HIM TO PUT ME OUT OF my misery and tell me what the hell this is all about. When he doesn't continue and I can't stand the silence any longer, I tell him, "Out with it, man! I'm getting all jittery."

"Okay, so earlier in the night, I overheard two guys talking about a woman they had both dated. They were saying how great things were in bed, then all of a sudden, it changed, and the relationship was over within a few months. That she kind of forced them to end it. Actually, it was more like they implied she manipulated the situation so they would want out."

Sam continues his story, but I'm no longer listening. Two guys discussing a woman they both dated for a few months. Dear God, he's talking about Paul and Brent. They were there that night. My embarrassing run-in with Brent plays out behind my closed eyelids. Sam only approached me because he thought I was a sure thing. I want to crawl into a hole and die.

"Hannah." Sam's voice drags me back into the moment.

My stomach churns, and I place an unsteady hand over it. "I think you should leave." I don't even want to hear the rest of what he has to say. My head starts pounding, and I get to my feet.

"No, please hear me out. I wanted to have this conversation with you before we were intimate, but it just didn't happen that way."

He reaches for me, but I pull away. "Don't touch me."

His hand drops back to his side, and the pleading in his eyes nearly breaks me.

"Did you seek me out because you thought I was an easy lay?" A bitter laugh bursts from my lips, because I totally was. I've never moved this fast before. "Well, congratulations, you got what you wanted. You can go now."

He shakes his head. "You're not listening to me. Yes, I wanted to sleep with you, but that's not all. You have no idea what it's like for a man like me to find someone to spend time with."

My eyes widen at his outrageous statement. "Are

you serious? Do you think I didn't notice the women practically drooling over you when we went out? You could literally take your pick," I scoff.

The deep blue of his irises flicker with annoyance. "Do you know how much I'm worth, Hannah?"

I roll my eyes. "I don't care about your stupid money, *Sam*."

"Exactly." He points at me. "You know, my last girlfriend faked a pregnancy to try to make me marry her. It had nothing to do with me as a person." He loosens a frustrated growl and runs his hands through his hair. "All I wanted was to be with a woman who doesn't give a shit about who I am and who wants to hang out and fool around for a while. And to not have to worry about her planning a future that has nothing to do with me and everything to do with my money."

I'm stunned into silence. For a whole minute, I just look at him, his words running on a loop through my head. I can feel my frown deepening as it all sinks in. "What the hell kind of women have you been dating?"

Like an invisible weight has been lifted from his shoulders, he shrugs. Light finally returns to his gaze. "The wrong ones, obviously."

"No shit," I blurt.

He chuckles then reaches for me again. This time, I let him take my hand, and his thumb caresses the underside of my wrist as he speaks. "I didn't tell you this to hurt you. I wanted you to know; I'm aware you don't want a long-term relationship, and I'm okay with that. But instead of things having to get bad or awkward between us, how about we make a deal?"

I arch my brows. "What kind of deal?"

"When either of us is ready for this thing we've got going on to end, we talk about it. Let's go out on a high note and part ways as friends."

That actually sounds really good. I smile at him then push onto my toes. "You have yourself a deal," I murmur against his lips, then I kiss him.

SAM

HER TONGUE PARTS MY LIPS, AND I WRAP MY ARMS around her tiny waist, drawing her body closer. I love the feel of her pressed against me. My dick starts getting the wrong idea as blood pumps south, and he begins growing in my trousers.

"Seriously?" Hannah pulls her lips away from mine, her eyes darting to my burgeoning hard-on.

I shrug. "He likes you as much as I do."

Dimples pop in her cheeks as she smiles, then she waggles her brows and lowers herself to her knees before me.

My eyes widen. "Holy shit. What are you doing?"

"What's it look like I'm doing?" she murmurs in a husky whisper that has my dick straining to get to her.

I release a pent-up breath. "You don't have to do that, Hannah." My dick is yelling at me to shut my damn mouth, but I had to say it.

She smirks. "Soon you'll learn, Sammy, I don't do anything I don't want to." Then, she lowers my zipper and frees my cock.

It throbs in her small hand. Her eyes meet mine as she leans forward and takes me into her mouth.

My fingers lock in her hair, and she sucks me to the back of her throat. "Christ," I groan.

Her free hand cups my balls, and she rolls them in her palm while massaging my taint with her fingertips. My hips surge forward—I can't help it—and then she moans—I definitely can't stop doing it.

Less than five minutes later, I come in her sweet mouth then help her back to her feet. A few strands of her long, pink hair hang in her eyes, and I tuck them back behind her ear then kiss her soundly.

When I pull away, she grins at me, and I know I'm mirroring it.

The next few days fly by with nothing more than a few texts shared between us as we're both busy with work. I'm anxious to see her on Saturday, but Friday afternoon, I get a text from Hannah, telling me she has to cancel our dinner.

To say I'm less than happy about it is an understatement. But she says it can't be helped.

It's a full week before we'll get to see each other in person again, but we've been video-calling almost daily. Which is what we're doing right now.

"And this is Leviathan," she chirps, turning her phone around to face a huge fish tank that I somehow missed when I was there the other week. "Levi, say hi," she tells the lobster.

I laugh. "Wow, I thought you were kidding about having a pet crustacean."

The phone whips back around to Hannah's face. She frowns. "Who would joke about having the best pet in the world?"

"I don't know," I say, chuckling at the confused expression on her beautiful face. "Are we still good for breakfast tomorrow?"

"Yep, I'll meet you at your fancy-ass building at five," she says, grinning. "Okay, I've gotta run. See you tomorrow, sexy pants."

She ends the call before I even get to tell her how awful the nickname is.

CHAPTER ELEVEN

SAM

HANNAH AND I CONTINUE TO SEE EACH OTHER FOR THE next few weeks whenever we can. Between my work at English Enterprises and Hannah's busy schedule at The Aquarium, it's hard to make time for each other, but we do.

It's mostly been breakfasts since we're both early risers who work long hours. We've squeezed in a couple more lunch dates in the back room at The Aquarium, as well. Then, Hannah came to surprise me at the office between meetings two days ago, wearing a fitted trench coat—and nothing else. . .

Tonight, we're finally having that dinner we tried for weeks ago. I'm waiting out in front of Alejandro's for her to arrive when none other than Camille strides past with her next potential husband. *Poor sucker.*

Upon noticing me, she pauses. "Samuel, what a

pleasant surprise. This is Marco Valentine. You've heard of Valentine Construction, yes?"

I roll my eyes. I've known Marco for years; we went to college together. I tip my chin in his direction, ignoring the viper at his side. "Careful with this one. She'll go to extraordinary lengths to lock you down."

"How dare you!" Camille screeches at the same time Marco takes a step away from her.

He eyes her before his gaze shifts to me. "Something I should know, brother?"

"Don't listen to him, Marco. He's just bitter because I ended things with him," Camille sneers.

An unladylike snort comes from behind her, and she spins to glare at the eavesdropper.

Hannah steps around her and over to my side, pushing onto her toes to press a kiss to my cheek. "Sorry I'm late, sexy pants. Traffic was a bitch."

My hand slides around her waist as I tug her closer and drop a kiss atop her head. "No problem, sweet cheeks."

Marco smirks, and Camille's jaw drops. "Who is *she*?" Camille demands.

I open my mouth to tell her to mind her business, but Hannah presses a hand to my chest, silencing me.

A sweet smile lights her face, and she steps forward, extending a hand to Camille. "I'm Hannah, the woman who doesn't have to fake a pregnancy to secure future dates with Sammy here."

Camille's eyes flare, and she launches for Hannah. I yank Hannah back behind me as Marco goes for Camille, wrapping his hands around her biceps and dragging her away.

He looks over his shoulder to me, eyes wide and questioning.

"I'll call you tomorrow," I mouth, and he nods his acknowledgment.

Almost a dozen eyes are on us now. *Great, just great.* "The spectacle is over. You may carry on with your evenings," I snap, and the small crowd disperses.

I turn to Hannah, taking in her beautiful face. She makes me feel so many things all at once. I have to grit my teeth to stop myself from saying all the things I know she doesn't want to hear because this is temporary.

The smile she was wearing fades at my expression. "Sam, wha—"

My fingers glide over her cheeks and into her hair. *Keep it light, Sam.* "You are all kinds of trouble, woman. What am I going to do with you?"

HANNAH

NERVES ZIP THROUGH MY BODY LIKE AN ELECTRIC current. The way Sam is looking at me. . .it's almost feral.

I lick my lips, and his gaze follows the action. "Umm, I don't know. Take me inside this fancy-ass restaurant and feed me?"

He shakes his head slowly. The glint in his eyes makes my lady-bits tingle in awareness. What is it with this man and his ability to turn the temperature up with just a look?

"Ah, Sam, are we going to go inside? It's awful hot out here . . ."

The corner of his mouth hooks in a panty-melting grin. "How did you know she's the one who faked the pregnancy?"

I shrug. "Lucky guess."

"And if it wasn't her? What would you have done?"

I shrug again. "Would it have mattered? The way she was talking down to you was enough to piss me off. Then I heard the little warning you passed on to her date and knew she'd definitely done something to deserve the look of distaste you were casting toward her."

"I see," is all he says.

I frown, and he removes his fingers from where they're buried in my hair to run his thumbs over the lines marring my forehead. "Watching you defend my honor was the biggest turn-on."

My grin is instant. "Everything turns you on, you horndog."

"Only when it comes to you. I'm not usually this bad. I swear. I'm sure if you give me a couple more weeks, he'll calm down."

Wrapping my hands around his collar, I tug his face to my level. "Now why would I ever want that?" I whisper over his lips then press mine to his.

His hands are back in my hair, tilting my head the way he wants it. I melt into his hard chest, loving every little bit of his attention.

He breaks the kiss, panting against my swollen lips. "I want to take you back to my place and show you just how much I liked that little show. But I promised you food, and I know how you feel about steak. This place has the best steaks in the city. So, I'll feed you first, then I'll feast on *you*."

His words stoke my already raging libido. "Okay," I murmur.

His hands drag over my neck, along my collarbone, then slide down my exposed arms to take my hands. "I like this dress," he says.

I look at my simple black, strapless dress and the shiny, red-bow belt at my waist that matches my killer heels. "Thanks. Now stop complimenting me so we can go eat."

Sam smiles and shakes his head slightly. "Yes, ma'am." He drops one of my hands and leads me inside the restaurant by my other.

The moment we step inside, all eyes are on us— or I should say, me. And not in a nice way, either. I swallow and look at my feet when one woman's remark meets my ears. "Oh, how sweet, English is slumming it with the help this evening. I heard she works at Thomas's new establishment."

Sam's eyes narrow on the woman, and she meets his stare head-on, no shame in her face. She meant what she said and doesn't care that I heard it.

It takes me a moment to decide how I want to deal with the crude, assessing judgment of the other patrons. I can either feel ashamed of everything I have worked so hard for, or I can straighten my backbone and show them their words mean as much to me as they themselves do.

Inhaling a deep breath, I raise my head high and smile directly at the woman. Then, I smack Sam's ass and say, "Lead the way, hot stuff. This two-dollar hooker wants a steak."

Mouths gape and murmurs ensue as Sam chuckles and tugs me to a table in a dark corner, far away from all the prying eyes.

As soon as we're seated and our drink orders have been placed, Sam looks at me and, yet again, shakes his head. "Trouble," he mumbles under his breath, a huge shit-eating grin plastered on his handsome face.

"What a lovely bunch of people you seem to know, Sammy. And their manners. . ." I wave a hand in the air. "I had heard the upper crust attend etiquette lessons as children. You can certainly tell."

"If I didn't know better, I might think that's sarcasm I detect in your tone, Miss Archer," he muses, finger tapping his chin.

I place my hand over my chest, aghast. "Why, Mr. English, you have offended me, sir. A true lady never uses such crude modes of speech."

He rolls his eyes. "Of course. My sincere apologies."

I chuckle and relax into my plush chair. The waiter appears with our drinks and requests our meal orders. I look to Sam as we haven't even opened our menus yet. He winks at me then hands the waiter the unused menus.

"My usual, thank you, Terrance, by two, please. And the crème brûlée for dessert."

"Very well, sir," Terrance says with a slight bow of his head, then he's gone again.

Over our delicious meals, we make small talk about the weather, my work, his work, and our respective upcoming schedules.

"So, I'm not going to be able to see you this week again?" Sam asks.

"I don't think I'll be able to get away during the day. Maybe we could do dinner one night?"

He smirks. "Or I could bring you lunch again? I did quite enjoy our lunch date this week."

"I bet you did!" I chuckle.

Sometime later, our plates are cleared, and the dessert is placed on the table between us. I stare at the delicate dish, and my mouth waters at the sweet caramel scent wafting toward me.

Sam laughs lightly. "I take it you approve of my choices this evening then?"

"Hell yes, I do," I tell him, smiling brightly.

"Everything has been wonderful, except for your taste in company—myself excluded, of course."

"To be fair, I don't have control over who else dines here," he says, digging a dainty silver spoon into the crème brûlée and offering it to me.

I lean forward, and he slides the spoon into my mouth. An embarrassing moan escapes me as the exquisite flavor bursts on my tongue.

The spoon clatters to the table. "And on that note, I think it's time to get the check," Sam announces.

"But the . . ." I point at the dessert.

"We'll get it to go," he says, raising one hand to signal the waiter while the other discreetly disappears under the table.

Terrance approaches, and Sam tells him, "We'll get the check now, please, and take the crème brûlée with us."

I wait till Terrance is out of earshot then ask, "Are you seriously that turned on you can't wait until we finish?"

He slides his hand over mine on the table. "Baby, if I have to watch you eat the rest of this crème brûlée,"—he gives my mouth a pointed stare—"we're not going to make it home. Besides, I'd much rather feed it to you while you're naked."

CHAPTER TWELVE

SAM

I have a very vivid imagination, and right now, it's giving me some fantastic ideas regarding Hannah and that crème brûlée.

A seductive smile tugs at her gorgeous mouth. "Why, Sammy, are you trying to tell me you have a kink that involves food?"

"I'm pretty sure I'd be open to anything as long as it involves you naked." I grin as a blush tints her cheeks.

Terrance returns with the bill folder and a small box wrapped with a white bow containing our dessert. I slide a couple of hundreds in, making sure to leave him a nice tip, then take Hannah's hand and lead her outside where my car is waiting.

My driver opens the door for us, Hannah scoots in, and I follow, tugging her into my lap as soon as the door closes behind me. "I've been waiting to taste you all night," I murmur against her slender neck.

She arches into me. "Then what are you waiting for?"

My hands glide up her smooth thighs under the skirt of her dress. I lick and suck the column of her throat, thanking God for back seat dividers, as I move her panties aside and dip two fingers into her pussy. She squirms in my lap, riding my fingers as I pump them in and out. I grip her ass with my free hand, squeezing the plump cheek.

"Yes," she moans, reaching to stroke me through my trousers.

"Give me your mouth," I demand. I need her tongue on mine. She dips her head, grazing her lips over my jaw then dragging her mouth along my throat. "I said, give. Me. Your. Mouth."

Her head pops up, lust burning in her eyes as I slam my lips over hers, devouring her. She sighs into the kiss, and I slide my fingers out of her dripping pussy to fumble with my belt. I can't wait any longer to be inside her. She reaches out, helping me free my cock, wrapping her little hand over my length as I pull a condom from my wallet.

"Hurry," she whimpers. "I need you."

Fuck yes.

I roll the rubber over my shaft. Hannah hovers above me as I align us, then she drives down hard and fast. My head tips back against the headrest as she rides me, pleasure sweeping through every nerve ending in my body. I tug at the top of her dress, her perfect breasts falling free, and I suck one of her rosy nipples into my mouth.

She shudders hard, sending shock waves through my dick as her body clenches around me. "Fuck, Hannah," I groan. "You feel so good, baby."

"Play with my tits, Sam. Keep touching me. I'm so close."

My hands snake around her torso, and I graze my fingertips over her ribcage then cup her breasts in my palms. "Like this, baby?" I ask, pinching her nipples between my thumbs and forefingers.

"Harder," she pants. "Harder, Sam! More . . ."

I drop my head and lightly trace my tongue around her nipple, not quite touching it, then bite it. Her body quakes, her pussy clenching around my cock like a vise as her back arches and I suck away the sting of my bite.

My dick throbs inside her, needing its own release. But she's spent now, her body slack, so I grip her waist and take what I need. I drive into her over and over until her core tightens around me again. I drop a hand between us and circle her clit, building her up.

"Sam, oh God, Sam," she cries.

The pad of my thumb finally presses on her little nub, sending her over the edge again and me along with her.

I POUR US A NIGHTCAP WHILE HANNAH WANDERS around my apartment, taking everything in. A little crease forms between her brows, and the urge to wipe it away has me moving toward her. "What's wrong?"

Her eyes sweep over the open-plan living and dining areas. "Nothing's wrong. It's just not what I expected."

My brows shoot up. "What were you expecting?"

"A little more life? I mean, the fish tank is cool. But the rest of this place is so . . . sterile." She shrugs.

I look around, trying to see it from her perspective. Crisp white walls, sleek black furniture, a few framed black-and-white landscape photographs adorning the walls, and an ultra-modern kitchen. "I guess it is a little sparse . . ."

She accepts the drink I offer then takes a seat on the couch and frowns again.

I chuckle. "What now? You don't like my couch?"

"It's awful. This is the most uncomfortable thing I've ever sat on."

Dropping beside her, it's like sitting on concrete. "Jesus, you're right."

She looks at me like I'm an idiot. "Did you not test it out before you bought it?"

I strum my fingers on my knee. "I did not. Actually, I didn't pick any of the furniture in here."

Hannah chokes on her port. "I'm sorry, what?"

"An interior designer decked the place out before I moved in," I explain.

She cringes. "You mean you paid someone to make your place this boring? You're a sucker, Sam. You got ripped off." Turning on the couch, she lifts her legs, placing her feet in my lap. "How long have you lived here?"

Throwing an arm over the backrest, I shift to face her. She looks so beautiful, her cheeks still flush from the quickie in the back of the car. Satisfaction pulses through my veins as my eyes skate over her now. She is so unlike any woman I've ever been with.

"Hello, Earth to Sammy boy . . ." She waves a hand in my face.

"Sorry, what was the question?"

She laughs lightly, and the sound hits me in the gut, just like it has every other time I've heard it. "How long have you lived in this monstrosity?"

I roll my eyes. "It's not that bad. I've been here for about five years."

Her eyes widen. "And it's looked like this the whole time? How can you stand it? This place is begging for some color."

"You brighten it up quite nicely."

She blushes and takes another sip of her port.

Taking one of her feet in my hands, I remove the delicate red heel then the other before running my thumb along her instep.

"Oh God, don't ever stop," she moans.

I laugh then do it again. She sighs happily and slouches into the corner. "This would be even better on a decent couch. Seriously, we need to do something about this thing." She pats the cushion beside her ass. "How, in five years, have you not noticed how hard it is?"

Shrugging, I continue to rub the soles of her feet. "I don't really sit on it. I mean, it gets used but not in the traditional sense."

Her eyes light with mischief. "Are you saying

what I think you're saying? You bone on this couch but don't sit on it?"

I nod. "Pretty much. It's a good height to bend a woman over the back of. Or to spread her out while I kneel on the carpet and eat her sweet pussy."

"Aha." Hannah squirms. "And how many other women have complained about the couch?" she asks in a breathy voice that shoots straight to my dick.

"None," I shoot back. "They were too busy coming to notice."

She arches a brow and tilts her head. "I'm trying to decide if I should be offended by the fact that you're taking the time to talk to me while we sit on this God-awful thing. Or if I should be pleased you actually want to talk to me."

My hands work their way over her calves as I continue to rub soothing circles into her muscles. "It's up to you how you want to take it." I grin. "But know that tonight is the first time I haven't been physically able to keep my hands to myself until I got home."

"So, I am special?" she muses.

"Very special," I murmur, my hands rising higher along her creamy flesh. "My recovery time is somewhat more impressive with you, too, even if I do say so myself."

Her dirty little smirk has me abandoning her legs, taking her drink from her and placing it on the coffee table. I offer her my hand, and she takes it, coming to stand before me, her fingers intertwined with mine.

"Want to be the first woman I fuck in my bed, Hannah?"

She licks her lips. "You don't do it in your bed with other women?"

I shake my head. "I have a spare room if I feel the need to use a bed. I don't like sharing my personal space. But I want you in *my* bed, tangled in *my* sheets. I want your scent to torment me for days after I've had you."

Hannah curls her hands behind my neck and jumps, wrapping her legs around my waist. "Then what are you waiting for?" she says and slides her tongue along my throat to my ear where she nips the lobe between her sharp teeth then sucks it into her hot little mouth.

I am rock-fucking-solid now. She has me so tightly wound I could fuck her where I stand. But I want her in my bed. Grabbing her ass cheeks in my palms, I stride down the hall to my bedroom.

HANNAH

THIS GUY IS GOOD FOR MY EGO. WHAT HE SAID ABOUT his recovery time isn't wrong. I've never been with someone who can rock it more than twice in a night. But Sam . . . we had sex at least four times that first night we spent together.

I continue to tongue his ear, loving how the hairs on the back of his neck stand up whenever I do it.

Once we're inside his room, he lowers me to my feet then takes a step *away from me*.

"Where are you going?" I ask, confused.

He walks backwards until he drops into a black leather wingback chair in the corner of the room. "Take off your dress for me, Hannah. I want to watch you."

Holy shit, he has some good ideas. I'm so turned on right now I could burst.

I undo the clasp of my little red-bow belt and drop it to the ground. Then, I turn my back to him, reach behind me, and slowly drag the zipper down my spine. I let the material pool at my feet and step out then spin to face Sam in nothing but my black-and-red lace thong.

He bites his fist, eyes riveted to my body.

"Like this?" I ask, stepping toward him.

He holds out a hand, halting me. "Take those off, too," he says, pointing at my panties.

Sliding my hands over my breasts, I take another step closer then drag them down my stomach. Sam's jaw clenches as I glide them around my hips before hooking my thumbs in the sides of my thong and, ever so slowly, shimmy them over my thighs. I drop them when I reach my knees.

"Better?" I smirk.

Sam's throat bobs as he swallows. "So much better." He stands before stalking toward me and curling his hand in my ponytail, yanking my head back. "Do you have any idea what you do to me?" he growls in my face.

"I have a fair idea," I tell him, reaching out to cup his hard length through his trousers. "Your turn," I say, stepping back, out of his reach.

His hand drops from my hair, a smirk spreading across his face as I turn my back on him and strut to his king-size bed. I climb onto it on all fours, my ass swinging in the air as I go, then I roll over on my side, waiting for the show.

"This isn't going to be fancy, just so you know."

I shrug. "You won't hear me complaining about a sexy beast getting naked for me."

His hand glides over the front of his dress shirt,

undoing buttons as he goes, exposing inch after inch of gloriously sculpted skin. When he reaches the bottom, he shrugs it off his broad shoulders to the floor. My mouth waters, and my pulse thunders as he unbuckles his belt while raising his gaze to mine, then tugs it free of his pants.

Instead of dropping the belt like I expect him to, he places it on the edge of the bed. I raise a brow in question. Sam simply grins. Then, he's tugging at his zipper, revealing black boxer briefs. Heat coils low in my belly as he dips his hand beneath the waistband and strokes himself.

I rub my thighs together then slide my hand between them, and he notices. "Uh-uh. You tortured me; now it's my turn. You don't get to touch yourself until I say so."

"But—" I start.

His hand stills inside his trousers. "Do we have a problem?"

I shake my head. "No," I pant. *What is it about him being a bossy-ass that turns me on so much?*

He smirks. "Good." His hand goes back to stroking his cock, but I want to see what he's doing.

"Take off your damn pants, Sam."

His eyes burn at my command. But he does as I say, dropping his trousers and boxers to the ground.

My fingers itch to touch—him or me, I don't care. I just need to ease this insistent hunger inside of me.

"You like watching me rub my dick for you, don't you, Hannah?

I nod vigorously. "Very much."

His head tips back as his fist squeezes his cock hard, and he groans. "As good as your eyes feel on me, your pussy feels better." Then, he's at the side of the bed, yanking open his top drawer and pulling out a box of condoms.

"Yo, Sammy—" The bedroom door flies open, smacking against the wall with a thud, leaving a slack-jawed Tom standing in the entrance.

I screech and roll to cover myself, but the bed linens are tucked in so damn tight I struggle to yank them free. *Oh-my-God! Oh-my-God! My-boss-is-staring-at-my-ass!* I give up on the blankets and fling myself off the side of the bed before peeking my head back to see what's going on.

Tom bursts out laughing, and I die of embarrassment, pressing my forehead to the side of the bed.

"What the hell?!" Sam yells at him.

Tom buckles over and slaps his knee as he wheezes through his amusement. "Oh my—" He gasps. "This is the best thing ever!"

I glare at him, and Sam stalks toward his cousin, still bare-ass naked. His penis slaps against his stomach with every step, then he shoves Tom out of the room. "What are you doing here?" Sam demands.

"I don't even remember why I came over." Tom chuckles.

CHAPTER THIRTEEN

SAM

THE FOLLOWING MORNING, I'M EATING BREAKFAST when Tom drops into his seat across from me at our table in Zenith's restaurant.

"Are you bringing Hannah to your birthday soirée next weekend?" he asks.

"I'd like to, but I don't know how that would play. I told you about her run-in with Camille at Alejandro's and the cold reception she got when we walked through the doors."

He sips his coffee then shrugs. "At least she'll make it interesting."

That's for sure. "As true as that is, I don't want to put her in a position where she's going to be ridiculed by a pack of spoiled, jealous bitches."

"Well, I've asked Amy. You're going to look like an asshole if you don't ask Hannah now," Tom states, smirking.

I glare at him. That fucker is going to screw this up for me; I just know it. "Why did you ask Amy? You two aren't even that serious."

He scoffs. "Says you—the man who's dating a woman for no-strings sex for a couple of months."

My fists clench on the table. I'm tempted to haul him over it and beat the shit out of him for talking about my relationship with Hannah like that. *But it's true, isn't it?* She and I agreed we'd only do this for a few months, then we would go our separate ways. The problem is, I'm enjoying my time with her more than I ever expected.

Now, we're nearing the two-month mark, and I can feel our time together slipping away the way money slips through Tom's fingers. But it's not what I want anymore.

Before Hannah, all I wanted was a woman who would be happy to see the back of me. Now, I just want her. *Fuck.*

My fingers strum the tabletop, and my jaw clenches. I don't know how to make her stay. How to convince her we can be *this* good for the rest of our lives. We're fucking electric when we're together. *Surely she feels that too?*

Tom kicks me under the table. "Loosen up. You

look like you're going to burst a blood vessel all over my amazing suit."

I finally take note of the suit he's wearing. It's dark-emerald green. "Another gem from Bobby's collection, I assume?"

He sips his coffee before answering me. "You know it. I've been saving this one. Amy said we might start exploring butt stuff tonight." He waggles his brows, and I laugh.

"And you think that suit is going to seal the deal for you?"

"Bobby said the green really makes my eyes pop."

I shake my head and pick the newspaper up, effectively ending this conversation with Tom as his breakfast is served. Not that I can concentrate on the words on the page in front of me. All I can think about is Hannah and what I can do to keep her in my life.

Maybe I should bring her to my birthday. It's the perfect opportunity to show her I want to make this a serious arrangement, and I don't give a fuck what high society has to say about it or her.

HANNAH

SITTING ON THE SIDE OF THE TANK, ON THE DIVE platform, with my legs dangling in the cool depths, I admire Tina gliding with effortless grace through the water. She's so beautiful my heart swells just watching her. How could people feel anything but awe when seeing such a magnificent creature? This is my happy place, my thinking place, my peace.

"Hey, what's got you looking so melancholy?" Vi asks, plopping beside me.

"Just admiring my girl and wondering how anyone could want to hurt her," I say, hoping to throw her off the trail of what's really bothering me.

Vi nods, then her shoulder bumps mine. "But what's really on your mind? You usually come here when something's up."

My head falls back, and I stare at the ceiling. *Why is she so perceptive?*

"Come on, Han. We've worked together a long time. I know your tells." She chuckles and wraps an arm around my neck, tugging me into her side. "You wanna talk about it?"

I shake my head. "Not really. It's just something I need to do, and I don't think I want to." I sigh. "But I *have* to."

"Way to be cryptic, dude," Vi says, rolling her eyes.

"Sorry," I mumble. "It's complicated."

"I'm going to go out on a limb here and say it's a guy thing, yeah?"

I nod, and she squeezes me closer. "You don't have to talk about it if you don't want to. You came to the right place to think, though. I chill out here, too, when something's bothering me. But if you change your mind, you know where to find me."

"Thanks, Vi. But there's nothing to talk about."

My feelings for Sam are getting out of control. It's time to pull back. Time to engage The Starfish Method.

When I finally get home, it's after seven, and Sam will be here soon. I flop onto my couch and heave a dramatic sigh as I tap out a text to Amy.

ME: I need to implement my Starfish Method sooner than later this time around.

Her reply is immediate and not at all surprising.

AMY: I don't think you should do this. I know you like him. Like, more than any of the other guys you've dated in . . . well ever.

She's such a romantic. She can't help it. I know

this, but it still annoys me that she doesn't understand why I have to do it. If I leave it any longer, he's going to own my whole damn heart, then he'll break it—just like every other man before him. I really need Amy's support right now, but I have a feeling I'm not going to get it this time.

ME: It's not about how much I like him, Ames. And you know it.

If it was, there's no way I'd be pulling the starfish out. I really, really like Sam. He makes me laugh; he's charming; he's sweet; and dear God, he's amazing in bed. The O's that man has given me will stay with me for life.

AMY: WELL IT SHOULD BE!

My eyebrows shoot up at her rapid response.

ME: Wow, shouty caps. I'm impressed. But it changes nothing. I have to do this. Sometimes a girl's gotta do what a girl's gotta do to protect her heart. 'Cause nobody else is going to do it for me.

AMY: Yeah, well, in the past I could understand why you felt that way. But Sam is different. You're so happy with him. And Tommy says he's never seen Sam happier either.

I can't do this with her, so I turn my phone off and put it in my bedside table. Yeah, Sam does make me happy. And we click, despite coming from completely different worlds. But it's not that simple —matters of the heart never are.

I've got a little while before Sam is coming over, so I go out to the living room and dig out Levi's pellets. I drop a few in his tank and smile as he scuttles out of his hidey hole to retrieve them. "You'll never break my heart, will you, buddy."

I swear he stops and looks at me. I give him a couple of extra pellets for his undying loyalty.

In the kitchen, I pull out the ingredients to make a quick pasta dish and get to work.

I'm pouring myself a glass of wine when a knock sounds from my front door, and I go to let Sam in. I invited him over for dinner with the intention of tonight being the night The Starfish Method is put into action.

When I swing the door open, it's not the smiling

face I'm used to being greeted with. Rather, he's frowning at his phone. I reach out, touching his bicep. "Everything okay?" I ask, genuinely concerned.

His head jerks up. "I don't know. Maybe you should tell me."

I'm taken aback by the sharp edge to his words. "What? I—what's wrong?"

He pushes past me into my apartment, going straight to my fridge where I've started keeping some of his favorite beer on hand. Taking one out, he pops the top then downs the whole thing and reaches for another.

I've never seen him like this before. I approach with caution. "Tell me what's going on with you."

He shakes his head, and when his eyes meet mine, they're . . . sad.

"Sam?" I step closer, reaching for him.

His fingers curl around my outstretched hand, and he tugs me into his hard body then kisses me soundly. I fall into it, letting him take what he so clearly needs from me.

His hands slide into my hair as he deepens the kiss and walks me backwards along the hall, all the way to my bedroom.

The back of my knees hit the edge of my bed, and I tumble onto it.

Sam hovers above me, determination blazing in his blue depths. "Come to my birthday celebration next weekend."

I shake my head but keep my mouth shut as I fumble with his belt. We'll be over by then. Only he doesn't know it yet.

His hand covers mine, stilling my progress with his pants. "I want you there, Hannah. I won't take no for an answer."

My throat thickens, and I shake my head again. "I can't," I murmur and finish unfastening his pants.

A frustrated growl ripples through Sam's chest, and he tugs my hands up, pinning them to the bed above my head. "Why?" he demands.

"I just can't."

His eyes narrow. "Can't or won't? 'Cause I haven't even told you when it is yet."

Crap.

I shrug. "I'm working the whole weekend next week." I'll have to swap some shifts around, but I'll make it happen.

Sam shakes his head and slams his mouth on mine. This kiss is different, demanding and possessive. It feels so good I never want it to end. I need to touch him. I pull my pinned hands, but Sam squeezes them tighter until I stop struggling.

"I want you like this. Don't move your arms," he says, and it feels as if he's staring straight into my soul.

I nod and he releases them, grazing gentle fingertips over my wrists, my forearms, and my shoulders. Then, he takes each side of the cute button-down dress I'm wearing and rips them apart, sending buttons flying and my desire for him soaring. I squirm beneath him as he tugs his shirt over his head and tosses it to the side then kicks off his pants.

Keeping his eyes on me, he takes a condom from the top drawer of my dresser and tears it open with his teeth then sheaths himself. My fingers twitch with the need to touch him, but I keep them where he left them.

He nods at my restless hands and grins. "Don't like not being an active participant?" he taunts.

There's something about his words that sends alarm bells ringing in my head, but I'm not sure what or why. I don't have time to think about it either as he drops to his haunches between my spread thighs and blows on my sex through my lace panties.

Holy mother of all things orgasmic. My back arches off the bed when he dips his head lower and glides his tongue over the delicate fabric. "Sam," I whimper, and my fists clench.

His deep-blue eyes flick to meet mine as he repeats the move again and again. I'm a wet, dripping mess by the time he's done. Relief rushes through my entire body when he finally takes my panties in hand and slides them down my legs to position himself at my entrance.

"Let me touch you," I beg.

Sam shakes his head. "No." And without another word, he thrusts his powerful hips, and he's buried deep inside me.

I'm filled with sensation as he sets his pace. In, out, in and out, grinding his pelvis into my clit with every drag back and forth. My body shudders, an orgasm building rapidly. Heat pools low in my belly, tingles shoot through my legs, and I lift them to wrap around his waist, but he stops me.

"Don't move, Hannah." He takes my thighs in his big palms and lowers them back to the mattress, spreading me wide. "Just lie there and take it," he growls.

Then, his thrusts turn feral. Hard, fast, and out of time. He pounds into me relentlessly, and I love it. My fingers dig into my comforter, clenching it in my fists as my orgasm ripples through me, and with a harsh growl, Sam follows close behind.

CHAPTER FOURTEEN

SAM

I KNEW SHE WAS GOING TO CALL OUR TIME TO AN END soon, but not this soon. Not yet.

"That was . . ." She pants, catching her breath. "What was that, Sam?" Her eyes scan my face, searching.

Licking my lips, I sit back on my haunches then reach for her hands still clenched in the blanket above her head. She tangles her fingers with mine and smiles at me, but I still feel the question in her eyes.

"That's what I think of your Starfish Method."

Her expression goes blank, and she blinks at me. "Excuse me?" she breathes.

I cock my head to the side. "I said, that's what I think of your Starfish Method, Hannah."

She turns white before my very eyes. The fresh pink blush that stained her cheeks a moment ago is long gone. She opens her mouth to say something, but I silence her with a kiss. I don't want to hear her words right now.

Stark relief fills my veins when she kisses me back. I honestly didn't know how she would respond. When I pull away, unshed tears glisten in her eyes. I smooth a palm over her cheek, resting my thumb on her plump bottom lip.

"If you think starfishing is going to turn me off, or send me away, you are so very, very wrong, baby. If you just want to lie there and enjoy what I give you, I can work with that. If you want to ride me like our lives depend on it, I'm good with that, too. But I am *not* good with you trying to get rid of me."

She swallows hard then squeezes her eyes shut. "Can you give me a bit of space for a second please?" she whispers.

I'm off her in an instant, rolling to her side.

She scrubs her face with her hands then takes a deep breath and sits. She reaches for the silk robe on the end of the bed before slipping it over her shoulders and wrapping it around her waist. Then, she turns back to face me.

"We need to end this. I'm sorry, but we have to."

"Why? We're so good together. Why would you want to throw that away?" I ask, so damn confused.

"Because you terrify me. You already have a piece of my heart after such a short time. If I don't walk away now, you'll have it all, and when you're done with me . . . I won't have anything left."

I don't know what I was expecting her to say, but that was not it. I close the distance between us and take her hands in mine. "Then stay with me, Han." Releasing one of her hands, I wipe away the tear clinging to her cheek. "I won't ever be done with you, baby," I vow.

But she shakes her head, even as she leans into my palm cupping her jaw. "I can't. And you will. I've been here before, Sam, and I don't have another heartbreak in me. You've obviously talked to Amy if you know about The Starfish Method. This is just what I need to do."

A sad smile tugs at the corner of her mouth, and I desperately want to kiss her sadness away. Then, she chuckles lightly, as if any of this is funny. "You've ruined it for me, if that makes you feel any better."

I frown. "Ruined what?"

"I'll never be able to pull a starfish again without thinking of you." She blinks rapidly as more tears gather on her lashes. "I actually think you've ruined me for all other men."

Satisfaction surges through me. "Good. That's

good. I don't want another man to touch you ever again. You're mine, Hannah. What do I need to do to show you I'm not going anywhere?"

She shrugs and sniffles. "Nothing. I don't think there's anything you can do to change my mind."

"Fuck that," I spit. Getting to my feet, I snatch my clothes and tug them on.

I pause at the door, turning to look at her one more time. "I'll figure it out. So get ready for me, baby, because when I want something, nothing can stop me. I will do whatever it takes."

THE NEXT WEEK PASSES PAINFULLY SLOWLY AS I SPEND every waking minute trying to come up with a way to show Hannah that she can't push me away like this. That as long as she still has feelings for me, I will fight for her.

"I've brought in reinforcements!" Tom announces, barging into my apartment.

Amy pokes her head out from behind Tom's back and waves. "Hi, Sam."

"Would you two go away? I'm trying to think," I grumble, not in the mood for the lovey-dovey shit they've been throwing in my face all week.

Tom rolls his eyes and makes himself comfortable on one of the bar stools at my kitchen counter. "We gave you time to work this out on your own, and honestly, man, I thought you would have cracked it by now. But the stress is obviously causing your brain to misfire, so we came to spell it out for you."

I shake my head. "What are you talking about?"

"Her sharks," Amy pipes up. "You need to go swimming with her sharks."

My heart stops dead in my chest. *Anything but that.* "Are you insane? How am I going to show her I love her if I'm dead?"

Amy's eyes bug out. "You love her?"

Shit, I think I do. No, I know I do. Otherwise, I wouldn't be considering this asinine plan of theirs.

HANNAH

SAM MORE THAN BLEW MY STARFISH OUT OF THE water; he blew it out of the stratosphere. And I still pushed him away. No other guy would turn it around on me like he did. He made the starfish something hot and amazing. Who knew that was even possible? I didn't, and I've been doing it for years.

What is wrong with me? Oh, I know. Assholes—they're what's wrong with me. I was so sure I had it all figured out. The starfish weeded out all the assholes. It sent them packing with very little effort on my part. But Sam? I don't think he's one at all. And not just because he turned my escape plan on its head.

Not even spending time with my girls has helped my morose mood these past few days. I'm back on the dive platform, watching Tina do her sharky thing, and the joy it usually sparks is just not there today.

"Mind if I join you?"

Sam's deep voice has my head whipping around so fast it spins. I must be more than dizzy, 'cause it looks like Sam is wearing a wetsuit. I blink a couple of times to clear my vision, but nope—he's still in a wetsuit. "What are you doing here?" I ask.

His face pales as he gets closer to the edge of the tank where I'm sitting and peeks over into the water. "It's hot out. Thought I'd, ah, go for a . . . umm." He swallows hard and clears his throat. "A dip. I thought I'd go for a dip," he says.

I snort. Always with the jokes, this guy. "Get serious." I laugh. "What are you really doing here?"

He licks his lips, steps out onto the diving platform with me, takes another deep breath, and then sits beside me, legs in the water. "I'm not joking." His voice cracks with the words.

Now that he's next to me, the sheen of sweat covering his brow and gathering on his top lip is unmissable. He's sweating up a storm and super white, too. "Sam, are you feeling okay?"

"Just dandy," he says and sways to the side.

I reach out and grab him, holding him upright and steady. "I think you need to see a doctor. Something is definitely wrong with you."

He shrugs me off. "I'm fine. I'm doing this, and you can't stop me!"

"Umm, okay. What is it you're trying to do? Kill yourself?"

His eyes widen. "See?" he yells over his shoulder. "I told you they'd eat me!"

What in the hell is going on? I get to my feet and turn around to find Tom's and Amy's heads sticking out from behind an air vent. "Would someone care to explain?"

Tom opens his mouth to speak, but a splash has

me spinning around to find Sam has disappeared. "Sam!" I scream, running to the edge of the platform. He's sinking. *Oh God, can't he swim?* I dive in after him. It takes four powerful strokes to reach him, and I wrap my arms around his torso and kick as hard as I can.

We resurface seconds later, and Tom helps me haul an unconscious Sam onto the platform.

"What happened?" Tom demands. "Did you push him in? The guy is just trying to show you he loves you, and you try feeding him to your sharks! What is wrong with you?" he yells as I clear Sam's airway and roll him on his side.

Sam coughs and hacks up water. When I'm sure he's done, I turn him back over and slap him as hard as I can.

He bolts upright. "What was that for?" he yells.

"For scaring the crap out of me, you asshole!" I yell back.

"Guys, guys, settle down." Amy's calm voice enters the fray.

"Oh, fuck off, Amy. What the hell are you even doing here?" I spit. She and I haven't spoken since she admitted to spilling the beans about The Starfish Method to Sam and Tom.

She huffs and crosses her arms. "This is the thanks I get for helping get the best thing that ever happened to you back? You're so ungrateful, Han."

Still crouched at Sam's side, I throw my hands in the air. "Would someone please tell me what is happening?"

Sam grabs my flailing hands and knots our fingers together. His wet hair drips in his eyes, and he smiles at me with so much tenderness my heart aches. "I love you, Hannah. I thought coming here and facing my completely reasonable fears, by swimming with your babies, would show you that. But maybe I should have just told you."

Tears pool in my eyes, and I sniffle, desperately trying to hold them at bay. "You were going to swim with my girls? For me?"

He nods then shrugs. "I guess I technically did swim with them. Even though I was unconscious, it still counts, and I'm never doing it again."

Joyous laughter spills from my lips, and I launch myself at him, knocking us both back into the tank. I wrap my arms around him and kiss him hard. He doesn't kiss me back until I whisper, "They're scared of the splashing, and they're on the other side of the tank by now. I promise."

Then, it's on. Sam's mouth crashes into mine, and we kiss like it's our first and our last.

"I love you, too," I murmur against his lips then lead him over to the submerged ladder and let the big scaredy-cat exit the tank first.

EPILOGUE

SAM

TWO YEARS LATER. . .

I HOVER OVER MY INSANELY GORGEOUS WIFE AND TRAIL kisses along her torso, paying extra attention to her sensitive breasts.

She sighs and rolls her hips into my hard-on. "Good morning," she mumbles sleepily.

"Isn't it?" I say before sucking a pink nipple into my mouth. Hannah simply hums her assent. I move along her body, drawing pleasured moans and sighs from her. Skimming my nose along her throat, I relish the little shiver that ripples through her.

Positioning myself at her entrance, I go to surge forward, but something occurs to me, and I pause.

"Why'd you stop?" she whines.

"Are you starfishing me right now?"

Her eyes pop open, and she laughs. "Seriously?" She shakes her head, grinning. "Sam, I'm tired and heavily pregnant. I couldn't wrap myself around you even if I tried."

The sound of her laughter still affects me as much as it did when we met. I fucking love it. "Just checking." I chuckle, and she reaches for my face, dragging it to hers so I can kiss her thoroughly.

THE END.

ABOUT THE AUTHOR

JB Heller is an average Aussie housewife and Mumma in her early 30's with a wicked sexy imagination.

She writes romantic suspense, contemporary romance and romantic comedy. All with a healthy splash of heat, intrigue and wit. You'll love her sinfully sexy alpha hero's and their feisty counterparts.

Monday to Friday you can find JB glued to her laptop weaving words or trolling Pinterest for her next potential muse. Come the weekend, it's family time. (And of course lots of reading and Netflix binges.)

Want to know more? Look JB up on Facebook or check out her website https://www.jbtheindie.com

 facebook.com/authorjbheller

 bookbub.com/authors/j-b-heller

 instagram.com/jbtheindie

 twitter.com/jbtheindie

Also By

VIPERS DEN NOVELLA SERIES

(COMEDIC ROMANCE)

Piper & Kade

Pixie & Jake

Tay & Nate

ATTRACTION SERIES

(ROMANTIC SUSPENSE COMPLETED SERIES)

Undeniable Attraction

Pure Attraction

Fierce Attraction

Morgan Sisters Duo (Prequel)

ALPHA ONE PROTECTION SERIES

(ROMANTIC SUSPENSE-SEXY BODYGUARDS)

Worth The Risk

Worth The Wait

Printed in Great Britain
by Amazon